PATTERN OF A MAN
& OTHER STORIES

PATTERN OF A MAN
& OTHER STORIES

JAMES STILL

gnomon

Cover photographs of the author
and his home by Dean Cadle

Library of Congress Catalog Card
Number: 76-45313

ISBN: 0-917788-00-1 (cloth)
ISBN: 0-917788-01-x (paper)

for Dean & Jo Cadle

CONTENTS

In those days everybody knew
everybody else, and knew what he was
doing, and what his father and grandfather
had done before him, and you even knew
what everybody ate; and when you saw
somebody passing, you knew where he
was going, and families didn't scatter all
over the place, and people didn't go away
to die in the poor-house.

Giovanni Verga,
The House by the Medlar Tree

MRS. RAZOR

"WE'LL have to do something about that child," Father
said. We sat in the kitchen eating our supper, though
day still held and the chickens had not yet gone to roost
in the gilly trees. Elvy was crying behind the stove,
and her throat was raw with sobbing. Morg and I
paused, bread in hand, and glanced over our shoulders.
The firebox of the Cincinnati stove winked, the iron
flowers of the oven throbbed with heat. Mother tipped
a finger to her lips, motioning Father to hush. Father's
voice lifted: —

"I figure a small thrashing would make her leave off
this foolish notion."

Elvy was six years old. She was married, to hear
her tell it, and had three children and a lazy shuck of
a husband who cared not a mite for his own and left his
family to live upon her kin. The thought had grown
into truth in her mind. I could play at being Brother
Hemp Leckett, climb onto a chopblock and preach to
the fowls; or I could be Round George Parks, riding
the creeks, killing all who crossed my path; I could
be any man body. Morg couldn't make-believe; he was
just Morg. But Elvy had imagined herself old and
thrown away by a husband, and she kept believing.

"A day will come," Elvy told us, "when my man's

going to get killed down dead, the way he's living." She spoke hard of her husband and was a shrew of a wife who thought only of her children; she was as busy with her young as a hen with diddles. It was a dog's life she led, washing rags of clothes, sewing with a straw for needle, singing by the half hour to cradled arms, and keeping an eye sharp for gypsies. She jerked at loose garments and fastened and pinned, as Mother did to us.

Once we spied her in the grape arbor making to put a jacket on a baby that wouldn't hold still. She slapped the air, saying, "Hold up, young'un!" Morg stared, half believing. Later she claimed her children were stolen. It wasn't by the dark people. Her husband had taken them—she didn't know where. For days she sat pale and small, minced her victuals, and fretted in her sleep. She had wept, "My man's the meanest critter ever was. Old Scratch is bound to get him."

And now Elvy's husband was dead. She had run to Mother to tell this thing, the news having come in an unknown way. She waited dry-eyed and shocked until Father rode in from the fields in middle afternoon and she met him at the barn gate to choke out her loss.

"We've got to haste to Biggety Creek and fetch my young'uns ere the gypsies come," she grieved. "They're left alone."

"Is he doornail dead?" Father had asked. And he smiled to hear Biggety Creek named, the Nowhere Place he had told us of once at table. Biggety Creek where heads are the size of water buckets, where noses are turned up like old shoes, women wear skillets for hats, and men screw their breeches on, and where people are so proper they eat with little fingers pointing, and one pea at a time. Father rarely missed a chance to preach us a sermon.

"We've got to haste," Elvy pled.

"Do you know the road to Biggety Creek?"

Elvy nodded.

Father keened his eyes to see what manner of child was his own, his face lengthening and his patience wearing thin. He grabbed his hat off and clapped it angrily against his leg; he strode into the barn, fed the mules, and came to the house with Elvy tagging after and weeping.

"Fix an early supper," he told Mother.

Father's jaws were set as he drew his chair to the table. The day was still so bright the wall bore a shadow of the unkindled lamp. Elvy had hidden behind the stove, lying on the cat's pallet, crying. "Come and eat your victuals," Mother begged, for her idea was to humor children and let them grow out of their notions. But Elvy would not.

We knew Father's hand itched for a hickory switch. Disobedience angered him quicker than anything. Yet he only looked worried. The summer long he had teased Elvy, trying to shake her belief. Once while shaving he had asked, "What ever made you marry a lump of a husband who won't come home, never furnishes a cent?" Morg and I stood by to spread left-over lather on our faces and scrape it off with a kitchen knife. "I say it's past strange I've not met my own son-in-law. I hunger to shake his hand and welcome him to the family, ask him to sit down to our board and stick his feet under."

Father had glanced slyly at Elvy. "What's his name? Upon my honor, I haven't been told."

Elvy looked up. Her eyes glazed in thought. "He's called Razor."

"Given name or family?"

"Just Razor."

"Ask him to visit us," Father urged in mock seriousness. "Invite him up for Sunday dinner."

Elvy had promised that her husband would come. She had Mother fry a chicken, the dish he liked best, claiming the gizzard was his chosen morsel. Nothing less than the flax tablecloth was good enough, and she gathered day-eye blossoms for the centerpiece. An extra chair was placed, and we waited; we waited noon through, until one o'clock. Then she told us confidentially, "Go ahead and eat. Razor allus was slow as Jim Christmas."

She carried a bowl of soup behind the Cincinnati stove to feed her children. In the evening she explained, "I've learnt why my man stayed away. He hain't got a red cent to his pocket and he's scared of being lawed for not supporting his young'uns."

Father had replied, "I need help—need a workhand to grub corn ground. A dollar a day I'll pay, greenback on the barrel top. I want a feller with lard in his elbows and willing to work. Fighting sourwood sprouts is like going to war. If Razor has got the measure of the job, I'll hire him and promise not to law."

"I ought never to a-took him for a husband," Elvy confessed. "When first I married he was smart as ants. Now he's turned so lazy he won't even fasten his gallus buckles. He's slouchy and no 'count."

"Humn," Father had grunted, eying Morg and me, the way our clothes hung on us. "Sloth works on a feller," he preached. "It grows roots. He'll start letting his sleeves flare and shirttail go hang. One day he gets too sorry to bend and lace his shoes, and it's a *swarp*, *swarp* every step. A time comes he'll not latch the top button of his breeches—ah, when a man turns his potty out, he's beyond cure."

"That's Razor all over," Elvy had said.

Father's teasing had done no good. As we sat at supper that late afternoon, listening to Elvy sob behind the stove, Morg began to stare into his plate and would eat no more. He believed Elvy. Tears hung on his chin.

Father's face tightened, half in anger, half in dismay. He lifted his hands in defeat. "Hell's bangers!" he blurted. Morg's tears fell thicker. I spoke small into his ear, "Act it's not so," but Morg could never make-like.

Father suddenly thrust back his chair. "Hurry and get ready," he ordered, "the whole push of you. We're going to Biggety Creek." His voice was dry as a stick.

Elvy's sobbing hushed. Morg blinked. The room became so quiet I could hear flames eating wood in the firebox. Father arose and made long-legged strides toward the barn to harness the mules.

We mounted the wagon, Father and Mother to the spring seat, Elvy settling between; I stood with Morg behind the seat. Dusk was creeping out of the hollows. Chickens walked toward the gilly trees, flew to their roosts, sleepy and quarrelsome. Father gathered the reins and angled the whip to start the mules. "Now, which way?" he asked Elvy. She pointed ahead and we rode off.

The light faded. Night came. The shapes of trees and fences were lost and there were only the wise eyes of the mules to pick the road when the ground had melted and the sky was gone. Elvy nodded fitfully, trying to keep awake. We traveled six miles before Father turned back.

A MASTER TIME

WICK JARRETT brought the invitation of his eldest son, Ulysses. "He's wanting you to come enjoy a hog-kill at his place next Thursday," Wick said. "Hit's to be a quiet affair, a picked crowd, mostly young married folks. No old heads like me—none except Aunt Besh Lipscomb, but she won't hinder. 'Lysses and Eldora will treat you clever. You'll have a master time."

Thursday fell on the eve of Old Christmas, in January, a day of bitter wind. I set off in early afternoon for Ulysses' home-seat on Upper Logan Creek, walking the ridge to shun the mud of the valley road. By the time I reached the knob overtowering the Jarrett farm my hands and ears were numb, my feet dead weights. A shep dog barked as I picked my way down and Ulysses opened the door and called, "Hurry in to the fire." I knocked my shoes at the doorsteps. "Come on in," Ulysses welcomed. "Dirt won't hurt our floors."

A chair awaited me. Before the living-room hearth sat Ulysses' cousins, Pless and Leander Jarrett, his brothers-in-law, Dow Owen and John Kingry, a neighbor, Will Harrod, and the aged midwife, Aunt Besh Lipscomb, who had lived with Ulysses and Eldora since the birth of their child. From the kitchen came sounds of women's voices.

"Crowd to the fire and thaw," Ulysses said, "and pull off your jacket."

"Be you a stranger?" Aunt Besh asked.

"Now, no," Ulysses answered in my stead. "He lives over and across the mountain."

"He's got a tongue," Aunt Besh reproved. And she questioned, "Was I the granny-doctor who fotched you?"

Ulysses teased, "Why, don't you remember?"

Aunt Besh said, "I can't recollect the whole push."

The fellows chuckled under their breaths, laughing quietly so as not to disturb the baby sleeping on a bed in the corner.

The heat watered my eyes. My hands and feet began to ache.

"You're frozen totally," Aunt Besh declared. "Pull off your shoes and socks and warm your feet. Don't be ashamed in front of an old granny."

"Granny-doctors have seen the world and everything in it," Ulysses said.

"Hush," Aunt Besh cried, and as I unlaced my shoes she said, " 'Lysses, he needs a dram to warm his blood."

Ulysses shrugged. "Where'd I get it?"

"A medicine dram. Want him to catch a death cold?"

"I ought to of got a jug for the occasion," Ulysses said. "We're all subject to take colds. I forgot it plumb."

"I'd vow there's a drap somewhere."

"This is apt to be the driest hog-kill ever was," Ulysses said.

8

"Humph," Aunt Besh scoffed.

I had my shoes on again when the wives gathered at the fire. Eldora took up the baby, scolding Ulysses. "You'd let it freeze. Its little nose is ice." And Ulysses said, "We men, we might as well allow the petticoats to hug the coals a spell. Let's get some air." We followed him through the front door, and on around to the back yard. The wind tugged at us. We pulled our hats down until the brims bent our ears.

Ulysses led us into the smokehouse. "Look sharp," he said, "and see what there is to see." We noted the baskets of Irish and sweet potatoes, cushaws and winter squash, the shelves loaded with conserved vegetables and fruits. "Anybody give out of table stuff," he went on, "come here and get a turn." Will Harrod glanced about impatiently, and Dow Owen uncovered a barrel. Ulysses said, "Dow, if you want to crack walnuts, the barrel is full." Pless and Leander Jarrett took seat on a meat box and grinned.

"Ah, 'Lysses," Will Harrod groaned, "quit your stalling."

"Well, s'r," Ulysses said, "I've got some sugartop here, but it's bad, my opinion. I hate to poison folks." The bunch livened. Pless and Leander, knowing where to search, jumped off the salt box and raised the lid; they lifted a churn by the ears. Will said, "Say we drink and die." Ulysses cocked his head uncertainly at me. I said, "Go ahead, you fellows."

A gourd dipper was passed hand to hand, and Will,

on taking a swallow, yelled joyously. Ulysses cautioned, "Don't rouse Aunt Besh. We'd never hear the last." The gourd was eased from Dow Owen's grasp, Ulysses reminding, "A job of work's to do. We'll taste lightly right now." A jar of pickled pears was opened to straighten breaths.

We returned to the fire and the wives laughed accusingly, "Uh-huh" and "Ah-ha." Leander's wife clapped a hand on his shoulder, drew him near, and sniffed. She charged, "The sorry stuff and don't deny it."

"Pear juice," Leander swore. "Upon my honor."

"You've butchered the swine quick," Aunt Besh said scornfully. No attention was paid to her and she jerked Ulysses' coattail. "Are ye killing the hogs or not?"

"Can't move a peg until the women are ready," Ulysses answered.

"It's you men who are piddling," one of the women reported. "We've had the pots boiling an hour."

Eldora spoke, "Who'll mind the baby? I won't leave it untended."

Aunt Besh said, "Don't leave me to watchdog it."

Pless's wife volunteered to stay. She was the youngest of the wives, sixteen at most.

"Aunt Besh," Ulysses petted, "you just set and poke the fire."

"Go kill the hogs," Aunt Besh shrilled.

"She's the queen," Ulysses told us.

"Go, go."

Ulysses got his rifle. "John," he said, "you come help." And they made off.

There being two hogs for slaughter we waited until the second shot before rushing toward the barn, men through the front entrance, women the rear. The hogs lay on straw, weighing between 350 to 400 pounds. The wind raced, flagging the blazes beneath three iron pots. An occasional flake of snow fell.

We men scalded the carcasses in a barrel; we scraped the bristles free with knives while the women dabbled hot water to keep the hair from setting. The scraping done, gambrels were caught underneath tendons of the hind legs and the animals hefted to pole tripods; they were singed, shaved, and washed, and the toes and dewclaws removed. Ulysses and John served as butchers, and as they labored John questioned: —

"Want the lights saved?"

"Yes, s'r," Ulysses replied.

"Heart-lump?"

"Yip."

"The particulars?"

"Nay-o."

"Sweetbreads?"

"Fling them away and Aunt Besh will rack us. The single part she will eat."

Will Harrod laid a claim: "The bladders are mine. I'll make balloons."

The shep dog and a gang of cats dined well on refuse.

The wind checked and snow fell thicker. The women hurried indoors, carrying fresh meat to add to the supper they had been preparing nearly the day long. Ulysses and John hustled their jobs, the rest of us transporting hams, loins, shoulders, and bacon strips to the smoke-house. No hog-kill tricks were pulled. Nobody had a bloody hand wiped across his face; none dropped a wad of hog's hair inside another's breeches.

John complained to Ulysses, "The fellers are heading toward the smokehouse faster'n they're coming back."

"We'll join'em in a minute," Ulysses said.

When I entered the living room Aunt Besh asked, "Got the slaughtering done finally?" And seeing I was alone she inquired, "Where are the others?"

"They'll come pretty soon," I said, removing my hat and jacket and brushing the snow onto the hearth. "We put by the sweetbreads," I added.

Aunt Besh gazed at me. Pless's wife clasped the baby and lowered her face. Aunt Besh said, "Son, speak while 'Lysses hain't here to drown you out. Was I the granny-doctor who fotched you into the world?"

"Aunty," Pless's wife entreated, "don't embarrass the company."

"Daresn't I ope my mouth?" Aunt Besh blurted.

I said, "Who the granny was, I never learned."

"Unless you were born amongst the furren I'm liable

to 'a' fotched you. I acted granny to everybody in this house, nigh everybody on Logan Creek."

Pless's wife blushed. She stirred in her chair, ready to flee.

"There's a way o' telling," Aunt Besh went on. "I can tell whether I tied the knot."

Up sprang Pless's wife, clutching the infant. She ran into the kitchen.

"I wasn't born on Logan," I explained.

"Upon my word and honor!" Aunt Besh cried. "Are ye a heathen?"

Eldora brought the child back to the fire, and she came laughing. The husbands tramped in, Dow walking unsteadily, for he had made bold with the churn dipper. Will dandled two balloons. Hearing mirth in the kitchen John asked, "What has put the women in such good humor?"

Aunt Besh watched as a chair was shoved under Dow, and she began to wheeze and gasp. Presently Ulysses queried, "What's the trouble, Aunt Besh?"

"My asthma's bothering," she said. "The cold is the fault."

"Why, it's tempering," Ulysses remarked. "It's boiling snow, but the wind's stilling."

"My blood is icy, no matter."

"I'll wrap you in a quilt."

"No."

"I'll punch the fire."

"Devil," Aunt Besh blurted, "can't you understand the simplest fact?"

Eldora scolded, " 'Lysses, stop plaguing and go make a cup of ginger stew to ease her."

Ulysses obeyed, and Aunt Besh raised her sleeves and poked forth her arms. "See my old bones," she whimpered. "There's hardly flesh to kiver'em. I need good treatment, else I'm to bury." Tears wet her eyes.

"Aunty," Will comforted, "want to hold a balloon?"

"Keep the nasty things out of my sight," Aunt Besh said.

Ulysses fetched the stew—whiskey in hot water, dusted with ginger and black pepper. Aunt Besh nursed the cup between quivering hands and tasted. " 'Lysses," she snuffed, "your hand was powerful on the water."

Supper was announced and Ulysses told us, "Rise up, you fellers," and Eldora said, "You'll find common victuals, but try to make out." We tarried, showing manners. Ulysses insisted, "Don't force us to beg. Go. Go while the bread is smoking."

After further prompting we trooped into a narrow gallery lighted by bracket lamps, which was the dining room. John hooked a wrist under Dow's arm, leading him. Aunt Besh used the fire-poker for a walking stick.

"Why don't you eat with us women at the second table?" Eldora asked Aunt Besh.

"I don't aim to wait," Aunt Besh said. "I'm starving."

We sat to a feast of potatoes, hominy, cushaw, beans, fried and boiled pork, baked chicken, buttered dumplings, gravy, stacks of hand-pies, and jam cake. Ulysses invited, "Rake your plates full, and if you can't reach, holler."

As we ate, laughter rippled in the kitchen. Leander's wife came with hot biscuits and her face was so merry, Leander inquired, "What's tickling you feymales?" She made no reply.

John said, "They've been giggling steady."

"We ought to force them to tell," Leander said. "Choke it out."

"If you'll choke your woman," John proposed, "I'll choke mine."

"Say we do," Leander agreed. "And everybody help, everybody strangle his woman, if he's got one. But let's eat first."

A voice raised in the kitchen. "You'll never learn, you misters." The laughter quieted.

"We'll make them pray for air," Leander bragged loudly. He batted an eye at us. "We'll not be out-sharped."

"Cross the women," Ulysses said, "and you'll have war on your hands."

"Suits me," Leander said, and Pless and John vowed they didn't care. Will, his mouth full, gulped, and nudged Dow. Dow, half asleep, said nothing.

Of a sudden the women filed through the gallery, their necks thrown, marching toward the fire. Only Eldora smiled.

Ulysses said, "You big talkers have got your women

mad. But I didn't anger mine, you may of noticed."

"Ah," Pless said, "they know we're putting-on."

"Eat," Aunt Besh commanded, "eat and hush."

Dow nodded in his chair and Ulysses arose and guided him to a bed.

While we were at table the wives hid the churn, and when they joined us in the living room later in the evening the four estranged couples sat apart, gibing each other. Ulysses tried making peace between them. The wives wouldn't budge, though the husbands appeared willing.

John sighed, "Gee-o, I'm thirsty," and his wife asked sourly, "What's against pure water?" "Hit's weaky," was the reply.

Finally Ulysses threw open the door. The wind had calmed, the snowing ceased. Moonlight behind the clouds lighted the fields of snow. Every fence post wore a white cap. Ulysses said, "Maybe the way to end the ruckus is to battle. Who's in the notion to snowball-fight?"

"Anything to win the churn back," Leander said.

"The churn is what counts," Pless baited, "the women don't matter."

"A fight would break the deadlock," Ulysses declared.

The four wives arose.

Will groaned, "I'm too full to move," and John testified, "I can't wiggle." Pless and Leander were as lief as not, yet Pless reminded, "Me and Leander are old-time rabbit rockers."

Ulysses urged, "Tussle and reach a settlement."

The wives pushed John and Will onto the porch and shoved them into the yard. "Get twenty-five steps apart," Ulysses directed, "and don't start till I say commence." He allowed the sides to prepare mounds of snowballs.

I had followed to witness the skirmish, as had Eldora and Dow's wife. Behind us Aunt Besh spoke, "Clear the door. Allow a body to see."

Ulysses yelled, "Let'em fly," and the wives hurled a volley. A ball struck Will's throat and he appealed to Ulysses, "Rocks, unfair." Aunt Besh hobbled to the porch, the better to watch; she shouted and we discovered the side she pulled for. Will and John fought half-heartedly, mostly chucking crazy; Leander and Pless, deadeye throwers, practiced near-hits, tipping their wives' heads, grazing shoulders, shattering balls poised in hands. The women dodged and twisted and let fly.

Will sat in the snow when the hoard of balls was exhausted, and John quit—quit and yanked up his collar. Leander and Pless stopped tossing and batted the on-coming missiles with their hands.

The women crept nearer, chucking point-blank. They rushed upon Will and before he could rise to escape had him pinned. They stuffed snow in his mouth and plastered his face. Then they seized John, a docile prisoner, rolling him log-fashion across the yard. And they got hands on Pless. Pless wouldn't have been easily caught had not Leander grabbed his shoulders and shielded himself. Leander stood grinning as snow was thrust down Pless's neck.

Leander's feet wouldn't hold at his turn. It was run, fox, run around the house, the women in pursuit. He zigzagged the yard, circled the barn, took a sweep through the bottom. They couldn't overhaul him. His wife threatened, "Come take your punishment, or you'll get double-dosed." He came meekly and they buried him in snow. They heaped snow upon him and packed and shaped it like a grave. He let them satisfy themselves until he had to rise for air.

The feud ended and all tramped indoors goodhumoredly, the wives to comb rimy hair, the husbands to dry wet clothes and accuse Aunt Besh of partiality. Hadn't Aunt Besh bawled, "Kill'em" to the women. An argument ensued, Aunt Besh admitting, "Shore, I backed the girls."

The husbands fire-dried, chattering their teeth exaggeratedly, and their wives had the mercy to bring the churn from hiding and place it in the gallery. The dipper tapped bottom as its visitors heartened themselves. Aunt Besh eyed the gallery-goers. "I got a chill watching you fellers," she wheezed.

Ulysses said, "I don't hear your gums popping."

"Are ye wanting me to perish?" she rasped.

18

Eldora chided Ulysses into brewing another ginger stew, and Aunt Besh instructed, "This time don't water it to death."

It was Leander who remembered to inquire, "Now, what was it tickled you feymales back yonder?"

The women turned their heads and smiled.

The night latened, and Aunt Besh dozed. Husbands and wives, reconciled, sat side by side. The balloons were kept spinning aloft. Apples were roasted on the hearth, potatoes baked in ashes, popcorn capped, and pull-candy made.

Past one o'clock Eldora made known the retiring arrangements. Aunt Besh would sleep in her chair, on account of asthma. Two beds in the upper room would hold the women, two in the lower provide for the men. Ulysses and Eldora, occupying the livingroom bed, could keep the child near the fire and attend Aunt Besh's wants in the night.

My roommates sauntered off. When I followed they were snoring. John, Will, and Dow lay as steers strawed to weather a blizzard; my assigned bedfellows were sprawled, leaving little of the mattress unoccupied. I decided to go sleep in front of the hearth, though I waited until the house quieted, until smothered laughter in the upper room hushed.

I found the coals banked, the lamp wick turned low. Aunt Besh sat wrapped in a tower of quilts and I thought her asleep. But she uncovered her face and spoke, "See if there's a drap left in the churn." I investigated, and reported the churn empty. She eyed me coldly as she might any creature who had not the grace to be born on Logan Creek. "I'll endure," she said.

SNAIL PIE

THOUGH Maw's face was pale with anger, she didn't speak until Grandpaw Splicer and Leaf and I pushed back our plates. Grandpaw went to the barn to light his pipe, and Leaf followed to ask about the rattlesnake steak Grandpaw claimed he once ate. I crawled under the house, squatting beneath the kitchen floor, listening. I had a mind to learn whether Pap was going to tell of catching me chewing a wad of Old Nine. Maw was as set as a wedge against tobacco. She wouldn't spare the limber-jim. I heard her heel strike the floor impatiently; I heard the rounds of Pap's chair groan in the peg holes.

"Your step-paw has to hush his lie-tales at the table," Maw said, her voice pitching high in her nose. "Since he's come a meal hasn't rested easy in my stomach. We ought to send him back to the county farm."

"Forty years a drummer," Pap said, "forty years of drumming the mountain counties. He's too old to change his ways." The leather of Pap's shoes creaked. "Without a line of big-eyed lies he couldn't have sold gnat balls and devil's snuff boxes. That's what he vows peddling. He's always been a big hand to tease, and means no harm."

"Every time he sticks his feet under the table he talks of pickled ants or fried snails. His idee of being funny.

The name of snails I never could stand, much less the sight of them. Why, my innards turn at the word. And that pipe, foul as a pig pen. I told him straight off a whiff of tobacco smoke sickens me. I warned him to keep it outside of the house."

"Paw's a right smart company for the boys," Pap reminded. In my head I could see him saucering his coffee and blowing across it. "Keeps them occupied, and from under foot. Before he came I couldn't go bird-hunting without them whining to be along." Bird-hunting was Pap's delight. Maw called it his foolishness.

Maw's voice dropped from anger to dull complaint. "Doty and childish, worse than a child. My opinion, his mind is slipping. Why, he might even teach the boys to smoke. I can't get Todd to say what he talks about to them, but Leaf once did. He told an awful thing about a mole."

"Ay, I figure Pap keeps a good eye on the boys. You'd not know they were wormy if he hadn't found out. And he offered to locate some boneset to purge them."

"I'm no witch to start brewing herb tea," Maw said. "A bottle of vermifuge from the store will do the job."

"Come spring," Pap said, "Paw can hoe the garden. Nothing and nobody will fight weeds like an old man. I'll pay him a little to keep him in heart."

"We promised to try him for a month," Maw said. "A single month, and not a day beyond." Her words were cold and level. "For three weeks he's been here, and he brings up the subject of moles, slugs, or fish bait every meal. I say you've got to speak to him. He'll quieten or go back to the county farm. The next time he mentions snails—"

Pap clapped his empty saucer against the tabletop. "You oughtn't be so finicky," he declared. He shoved back his chair and got up. I heard dishes clink fit to break. "I hate like rip to call the old man down. I hate to." And then, anger rising, he blurted, "Putting one's kin in the poorhouse is a lately-happening business. A scandal shame! For all time past the agey have been cared for at home, pampered in their last days, indulged and cherished."

"If you'd heard what he told Leaf," Maw countered, her voice shrill. Pap's hand was surely twisting the door knob. "If you'd heard—"

Pap slammed the door so fiercely the skillets rattled behind the stove.

I hurried from under the house and ran to the barn. Leaf stalked the calf lot on johnny-walkers Grandpaw Splicer had made for him. Grandpaw sat in the crib whittling a cob, smoking and chewing. He was shaping a new pipe bowl with his barlow knife.

"Grandpaw," I said, "you never did tell me about that mole."

Grandpaw Splicer's eyes rounded, questioning. "Mole?" he made strange.

"You told Leaf," I reminded, acting slighted.

"Ah, yes," Grandpaw said, "what some fellers done with a mole varmint."

He blew a tobacco cud onto a shuck. He knocked pipe ashes into a crack. Then he opened his mouth suddenly, stuck out his tongue, and drew it back in, exploring. "By the gods!" he said, "I've lost another tooth." He spied into the shuck, and there it was. He pulled out his false plate to inspect the gap in it. "I need me a new set of teeth, but I've no money. It would take many a frog skin. Before long I'll have to gum my food and tobacco."

"I heard Pap say he was aiming to pay you a wage," I said. "I did, now."

"Ho!" Grandpaw breathed. The blue flecks in his watery eyes shone. "Ah!" He looked almost happy. He pitched the tooth into a poke of seed corn and said, "There's one grain that will never sprout." And he began to whack at the nub of the cob in earnest. A kink of smoke twisted from his pipe and the crib filled with the mellow smell of tobacco, ripe and sweet and pungent.

I watched the shaping of the cob, drawing in deep breaths of burning tobacco. "Grandpaw," I said, "I wish you were making that'un for me."

Grandpaw grunted, clicking his dental plates. "I knowed of a baby once was learnt to smoke in the cradle. Rather to draw on a pipe than his mammy's tit. Gee-o, if that little'un didn't grow up to be six feet and

24

weighed two hundred pounds. Tobacco was good for his constitution."

"I've been smoking a spell," I confessed.

Grandpaw chuckled. "I figured it was you who slobbered on my pipe stem yesterday. That's why I'm whittling a new one."

"Be the old'un for me?" I questioned, hoping.

"Now, no," Grandpaw said, "your mommy hates tobacco like the Devil hates Sunday. She'd hustle me back to the county farm before sundown did I give it to you. But if there comes a day you're bound to smoke, just steal this'un I'm making. I never relished anybody using my regular pipe. People oughten to smoke after each other. Onhealthy."

The bowl of the pipe was nearly finished. Only the marrow of the cob lacked scraping.

"Grandpaw," I said, "I'm scared you're a-going to be sent back. I heard Mommy talking."

"Hear!" Grandpaw chuffed. He put the barlow down slowly and the pipe bowl fell from his hand. He dipped into the seed corn, filling the pan of his hand with grains, lifting, pouring. His lower lip stuck out blue and swollen, the gray bag of his chin quivered. "Todd," he spoke, "you tell me exactly what your mommy said and I'll chop you out a pair of johnny-walkers like your brother's."

"I choose that pipe," I bargained.

"I'd rather to die than go back," Grandpaw moaned.

"Folks there perished already, just won't give up and lay down. Coffin boxes waiting in the woodshop. A pure death house. Ay, it's cruel. Cruel like what fellers done with a mole once." His eyes dampened, his hands shook, scattering corn. "You know what some jaspers done? They started a mole in the rear end of a bull yearling. That bully ran a mile, taking on terrible, and fell stone down dead."

"I'll keep the pipe 'tater-holed," I assured. "Nary an eye shall touch it."

"I long to stay on here."

I peeped through the cracks to see that no one was about. Leaf tramped the far side of the lot on his walkers. I told Grandpaw what Mommy had said and he listened, an arm elbow-deep in the corn sack. "Never tell Leaf nary a nothing," I warned. "He's bad to repeat. Just six years old, and he doesn't know any better. And don't mention snails."

"I'll play quiet-Bob," Grandpaw said. "By jacks, I will."

We heard Leaf coming *crockety-crock* on his johnny-walkers. He stuck his head in through the door. "Grandpaw," he yelled, his mouth curling with mischief, "did you ever eat a horse apple?"

On Saturday Pap went bird-hunting, and there were quails' breasts for dinner, and gravy brown as cured burley. We sat at the table watching Maw cut the breasts in half. She served her plate and passed the dish. Leaf

26

and I had been starved for two days, having taken the vermifuge Thursday and forbidden to eat a bite since. We could hardly wait longer. Our stomachs were about grown together.

Pap grinned at the dish. The breasts were no larger than a child's fist. His jaws set with pride. He had brought down three birds with one of his shots, bagged nine altogether; and he had prepared them as well, for Maw would never clean a fowl. He glanced at Grandpaw, seeking a good word for his prowess. "Three with one shot," Pap boasted. "You hear me? Three!"

Grandpaw's teeth clicked. His lower lip puckered, and I knew he had thought of something to tell. He raised grizzly eyebrows, wondering if he dared.

"One blast, three bobs," Pap crowed. "And that's no fish tale." His mouth smacked. "Ever see such mud-fat ones?"

"Hit was quare how I killed a bob-white once," Grandpaw related. He spoke slowly, picking his words, being careful. "Years ago when I lived in the head of Jump Up Hollow I went a-fishing on Shikepoke Creek. I caught so plagued many I had no place to put'em. I just shucked off my breeches, tied knots in the leg-ends, and filled'em with the prettiest redeyes and bigmouth bass ever was. So many fish I had to pack that a button popped off. And dadburn if that button didn't fly off and kill a bob-white."

"Sounds like the truth to me," Pap laughed. "I believe ever word." He winked at Maw. She had stopped eating, uncertain. Then she took another bite. Maw did mortally relish partridge.

Leaf spoke, his mouth full. "Grandpaw, where is Jump Up Hollow? I be to go there."

"Ah," Grandpaw said, poking a lip out. "Why, hit's so far backside of nowhere folks have to use 'possums for yard dogs and owls for rooster."

"I bet that hain't the truth," Leaf said.

"Swear to my thumb to my dum," Grandpaw said.

"I know me a tale and it shore happened," Leaf said. His eyes lit. He glanced at me and Grandpaw. I got a grain fidgety, for Leaf was bad to tittle-tattle.

"Truth?" Maw asked doubtfully. "I say keep it for another occasion. Truth won't spoil." And she served her plate again.

"Hear me," Grandpaw said, thinking back into his skull for another yarn. "It wasn't always good times in Jump Up Hollow. Once a hard winter come. Ninety days snowfall, ninety days hovering zero. Well, s'r, I gave out of bread and I gave out of meat. Not a lick of sweetening was left in the 'lassy barrel. Not a speck of nothing to eat the size of the chinebone of a gnat."

Maw laid her fork down, waiting. Her mouth was full, but she didn't swallow. I tried to catch Grandpaw's eyes but he was carried away in his telling. He paid me no mind. He lifted a hand, laying off the story-piece. I tried to poke him with a foot under the table but my leg wasn't long enough.

"Well, now," Grandpaw went on, "I got my old hog-rifle and searched the woods. Not a sight or sound of beast or varmint could I see or hear. But hell-o! In the sky there was a buzzard flying. I took hair aim and fetched him down with a single crack, and I 'gin to rip the feathers."

Pap opened his mouth to laugh, but Maw stared angrily at him. She had paled; her lips were tight against her teeth. Pap gulped, undecided. I slid low in my chair and kicked Grandpaw's knee. He grunted. He glanced at me in a fashion to let me understand he wasn't getting carried away.

"Did you cook that there buzzard?" Leaf asked.

"Now, no," Grandpaw replied. "I gathered the hungry smell in the meat box, mixed it with frost bite, and fried it with a smidgen of axle grease. Hit made good eating."

Maw swallowed at last. She stared at the victuals in her plate. I felt relieved, though I wished Grandpaw had played quiet-Bob as he had promised.

"I know me a tale," Leaf said, "and hit's the truth. I be to tell it."

"The truth?" Maw asked sharply.

"Gourd-head and tell," Pap joked. I could see he was glad Grandpaw hadn't eaten the buzzard.

"Be certain it is the truth," Maw warned, her voice pitching high and thin. "We could do with some honest speaking."

Grandpaw lifted his chin. He was a whet anxious.

"It was this morning," Leaf began. "That there worm medicine was pinching my stomach."

Maw grasped the tabletop. Her knuckle whitened; her face blanched the color of dough.

"I went in behind the barn," Leaf went on, "and there was Grandpaw and Todd a-smoking. Todd smoking a cob pipe Grandpaw made for him, a-blowing smoke big as Ike Pike. I be to have me a pipe too."

Grandpaw's chin quivered. His shoulders sagged, and he leaned forward and his eyes overflowed. Tears coursed the wrinkles of his cheeks, and he seemed old, old.

Leaf stared and hushed. He couldn't think why Grandpaw Splicer wept. His lips trembled. "Grandpaw," he said, trying to patch the hurt, "did you ever eat a snail pie?"

A RIDE ON THE SHORT DOG

WE flagged the bus on a curve at the mouth of Lairds Creek by jumping and waving in the road and Dee Buck Engle had to tread the brake the instant he saw us. He wouldn't have halted unless compelled. Mal Dowe and I leaped aside finally, but Godey Spurlock held his ground. The bus stopped a yard from Godey and vexed faces pressed the windows and we heard Old Liz Hyden cry, "I'd not haul them jaspers."

Dee Buck opened the door and blared, "You boys trying to get killed?"

We climbed on grinning and shoved fares to Roscoe into his hand and for once we didn't sing out, To Knuckle Junction, and Pistol City, and Two Hoots. We even strode the aisle without raising elbows to knock off hats, having agreed among ourselves to sort of behave and make certain of a ride home. Yet Dee Buck was wary. He warned, "Bother my passengers, you fellers, and I'll fix you. I've put up with your mischief till I won't."

That set Godey and Mal laughing for Dee Buck was a bluffer. We took the seat across from Liz Hyden and on wedging into it my bruised arm started aching. Swapping licks was Godey's delight.

The bus wheezed and jolted in moving away, yet we

spared Dee Buck our usual advice: Feed her a biscuit
and see will she mend, and, Twist her tail and teach her
some manners. The vehicle was scarcely half the length
of a regular bus. "The Short Dog" everybody called it.
It traveled from Thacker to Roscoe and back twice a
day. Enos Webb occupied the seat in front and Godey
greeted, "Hey-o, chum. How's your fat?" Enos tucked
his head, fearing a rabbit lick, and he changed his seat.
He knew how Godey served exposed necks. Godey
could cause you to see forked lightning and hear thunder
balls. Though others shunned us, Liz Hyden gazed in our
direction. Her eyes were scornful, her lips puckered
sour. She was as old as a hill.

Godey and Mal couldn't sit idle. They rubbed the
dusty panes with their sleeves and looked abroad and
everything they saw they remarked on: hay doodles in
Alonzo Tate's pasture, a crazy chimney leaning away
from a house, long-johns on clotheslines. They kept a
count of the bridges. They pointed toward the mountain ahead, trying to fool, calling, "Gee-o, looky yonder!" But they couldn't trick a soul. My arm throbbed
and I had no notion to prank, and after a while Godey
muttered, "I want to know what's eating you."

"We'd better decide what we can do in town," I
grouched. Roscoe folk looked alive at sight of us. And
except for our return fares we hadn't a dime. The pool-
room had us ousted. We'd have to steer clear of the
courthouse where sheriffs were thick. And we dare
not rouse the county prisoners again. On our last trip

we had bellowed in front of the jail, "Hey-o, you wife-beaters, how are you standing the times?" We'd jeered and mocked until they had begged the turnkey to fetch us inside, they would notch our ears, they would trim us. The turnkey had told them to be patient, we'd get in on our own hook.

Godey said, "We'll break loose in town, no two ways talking."

I gloomed, "The Law will pen us for the least thing. We'll be thrown in amongst the meanest fellers who ever breathed."

Godey screwed his eyes narrow. "My opinion, the jailbirds have you scared plumb. You're ruint for trick-pulling." He knotted a fist and hit me squarely on my bruise.

My arm ached the fiercer. My eyes burned and had I not glanced sideways they'd come to worse. "Now, no," I said; but Godey's charge was true.

"Well, act like it," he said. "And pay me."

I returned the blow.

Old Liz was watching and she blurted, "I swear to my Gracious. A human being can't see a minute's peace."

Godey chuckled, "What's fretting you old woman?"

"Knock and beat and battle is all you think on," she snorted.

"We're not so bad we try to hinder people from riding the bus," he countered. "Aye, we heard you squall back yonder."

Old Liz's lips quivered, her veiny hands trembled.

33

"Did I have the strength to reach," she croaked, "I'd pop your jaws. I'd addle you totally."

Godey thrust his head across the aisle and turned a cheek. He didn't mind a slap. "See your satisfaction," he invited.

"Out o' my face," she ordered, lifting her voice to alert Dee Buck. She laced her fingers to stay their shaking.

Dee Buck adjusted the rear-view mirror and inquired, "What's the matter, Aunt Liz?"

"It's these boys tormenting me," she complained. "They'd drive a body to raving."

Dee Buck slowed. "I told you fellers—"

"What've we done now?" Godey asked injuredly.

"Didn't I say not to bother my passengers?"

"I never tipped the old hen."

"One more antic and off you three go."

Godey smirked. "Know what?" he blatted. "We've been treating you pretty and you don't appreciate it. Suit a grunt-box, you can't."

"You heard me," Dee Buck warned.

When the bus stopped for a passenger at the mouth of Willow Branch Dee Buck called back to Aunt Liz. "How are ye, Aunty?"

"Doing no good," said Aunt Liz.

The twins got on at Lucus. They were about nine years old, as alike as two peas, and had not a hair on their heads. Their polls were shaven clean. Godey chirruped, "Gee-o, look who's coming," and he beckoned them to the place quitted by Enos Webb. Dee Buck seated the two up front and Godey vowed, "I'll trap the chubs, just you wait," and he made donkey ears with his hands and brayed. The twins stared, their mouths open.

Mal suggested, "Why don't we have our noggins peeled?"

"Say we do," laughed Godey, cocking a teasing eye on me. "They can't jail us for that shorely."

I replied, "We're broke as grasshoppers, keep in mind."

It didn't take Godey long to entice the twins. He picked nothings out of the air and chewed them, chewed to match sheep eating ivy; he feigned to pull teeth, pitch them back into his mouth, to swallow. The twins stole a seat closer, the better to see, and then two more. Directly Godey had them where he wanted. He greeted: "Hey-o, Dirty Ears."

The twins nodded, too shy to answer.

"What is you little men's names?" he asked.

They swallowed timidly, their eyes meeting.

"Ah, tell."

"Woodrow," ventured one: "Jethro," said the other. They were as solemn as fire pokers.

"Hustling to a store to spend a couple of nickels, I bet."

35

"Going to Cowen," said one. "To Grandpaw's," said his image.

"Well, who skinned you alive, I want to know?"

"Pap," they said.

Godey gazed at their skulls, mischief tingling him. He declared, "Us fellers aim to get cut bald in Roscoe. Too hot to wear hair nowadays."

I slipped a hand over my bruise and crabbed, "I reckon you know haircuts cost money in town." Plaguing Godey humored me.

"Witless," Godey said, annoyed, "we'll climb into the chairs, and when the barbers finish we'll say, 'Charge it to the sand bank.' "

"They'd summons the Law in an eye-bat."

"Idjit," he snapped, "people can't be jailed for a debt." Yet he wouldn't pause to argue. He addressed the twins: "You little gents have me uneasy. There are swellings on your noggins and I'm worried on your behalf."

The twins rubbed their crowns. They were as smooth as goose eggs.

"Godey's sharp on this head business," said Mal.

"Want me to examine you and figure out your ailment?" asked Godey.

The twins glanced one to the other. "We don't care," said one.

Godey tipped a finger to their heads. He squinted and frowned. And then he drew back and gasped, "Oh-oh!" He punched Mal and blabbed, "Do you see what I do? Horns, if ever I saw them."

36

"The tom truth," Mal swore.

"Sprouting horns like bully-cows," Godey said. "Budding under the skin and ready to pip."

"You're in a bad way," Mal moaned.

"In the fix of a boy on Lotts Creek," Godey said. "He growed horns, and he turned into a brute and went hooking folks. Mean? Upon my word and honor, the bad man wouldn't claim him."

"A feller at Scuddy had the disease," Mal related. "Kept shut up in a barn, he was, and they fed him hay and cornstalks, and he never tasted table food. I saw him myself, I swear to my thumb. I saw him chewing a cud and heard him bawl a big bawl."

Godey sighed. "The only cure is to deaden the nubs before they break the skin."

"And, gee-o, you're lucky," Mal poured on. "Godey Spurlock is a horn-doctor. Cured a hundred, I reckon."

"O, I've treated a few," admitted Godey.

"Spare the little masters," pled Mal.

Dee Buck was trying to watch both road and mirror, his head bobbing like a chicken drinking water. Old Liz's eyes glinted darkly. I poked Godey, grumbling, "Didn't we promise to mind ourselves?" But he went on:

"They may enjoy old long hookers, may want to bellow and snort and hoof up dirt."

"We don't neither," a twin denied.

Godey brightened. "Want me to dehorn you?"

The boys nodded.

Though I prodded Godey's ribs, he ignored me. He

37

told the twins, "The quicker the medicine the better the cure," and he made short work of it. Without more ado he clapped a hand on each of their heads, drew them wide apart, and bumped them together. The brakes began to screech and Old Liz to fill the bus with her groans. The twins sat blinking. Dee Buck halted in the middle of the road and commanded: "All right, you scamps, pile off."

We didn't stir.

"You're not deaf. Trot."

"Deaf in one ear, and can't hear out of the other'n," Godey jested.

Dee Buck slapped his knee with his cap. "I said Go."

Old Liz was in a fidget. "Get shut of them," she rasped her arms a-jiggle, her fingers dancing. "See that they walk. Make'em foot it."

"Old Liz," Godey chided, "if you don't check yourself you're liable to fly to pieces."

"Rid the rascals," she shrilled to Dee Buck. "Are ye afraid? Are ye man enough?"

Godey scoffed, "He'll huff and he'll puff—all he ever does. He might as well feed the hound a sup of gas and get traveling."

Dee Buck blustered, "I've had a bait of you fellers. I'm offering you a chance to leave of your own free will."

"Collar and drag'em off," Old Liz taunted. "A coward, are ye?"

38

"Anybody spoiling to tussle," Godey challenged, "well, let'em come humping."

Dee Buck flared, "Listen, you devils, I can put a quietus on you and not have to soil my hands. My opinion, you'll not want to be aboard when I pull into town. I can draw up at the courthouse and fetch the Law in two minutes."

"Sick a sheriff on us," Godey said, "and you'll wish to your heart you hadn't. We paid to ride this dog."

"Walk off and I'll return your fares."

"Now, no."

"I won't wait all day."

"Dynamite couldn't budge us."

Dee Buck swept his cap onto his head. He changed gear, readying to leave. "I'm willing to spare you and you won't have it."

"Drive on, Big Buddy."

The bus started and Old Liz flounced angrily in her seat. She turned her back and didn't look round until we got to Roscoe.

We crossed two bridges. We passed Hilton and Chunk Jones's sawmill and Gayheart and Thorne. Beyond Thorne the highway began to rise. We climbed past the bloom of coal veins and tipples of mines hanging the slope; we mounted until we had gained the saddle of the gap and could see Roscoe four miles distant. Godey and Mal cut up the whole way, no longer trying to behave. They hailed newcomers with, "Take a seat

39

and sit like you were at home, where you ought to be," and sped the departers, "I'll see you later, when I can talk to you straighter." The twins left at Cowen and Godey shouted, "Good-by, Dirty Ears. Recollect I done you a favor." We rolled through the high gap and on down the mountain.

I nursed my hurt and sulked, and eventually Godey growled, "I want to know, did you come along just to pout?"

"You've fixed us," I accused bitterly, and I openly covered my crippled arm.

Godey scoffed, "Dee Buck can't panic me. You watch him turn good-feller by the time we reach town, watch him unload in the square the same as usual. Aye, he knows what suits his hide." He grabbed loose my arm and his fist shot out.

It was too much. My face tore up, my lips quivered and tears smeared my cheeks. Godey stared in wonder. His mouth fell open. Mal took my part, rebuking him, "No use to injure a person."

"I don't give knocks I can't take myself," Godey said; and he invited, "Pay me double. Hit me a rabbit lick, I don't care. Make me see lightning." He leaned forward and bared his neck.

I wiped the shameful tears, thinking to join no more in Godey's game.

"Whap him and even up," Mal said. "We're nearly to the bottom of the mountain."

"Level up with me," said Godey, "or you're no crony of mine. You'll not run with my bunch."

I shook my head.

"Hurry," said Mal. "I see town smoking."

I wouldn't.

Mal advised Godey, "Nettle him. Speak a thing he can't let pass. Make him mad."

Godey said, "Know what I'm in the opinion of? Hadn't it been for Mal and me you'd let Dee Buck bounce you off the bus and never lifted a finger. You'd have turned chicken."

"I'd not," I gulped.

"Jolt him," Mal urged. "What I'd do."

"You're a chicken leg," Godey said, "and everybody akin to you is a chicken leg, and if you're yellow enough to take that I'll call you 'Chicken Leg' hereinafter."

I couldn't get around Godey. Smite him I must, and I gripped a fist and struck as hard as I could in close quarters, mauling his shoulder.

"Is that your best?" he belittled. "Anyhow, didn't I call for a rabbit lick? Throw one and let me feel it; throw one, else you know your name." Again he leaned and exposed his neck.

"He's begging," Mal incited.

I would satisfy him, I resolved, and I half rose to get elbowroom. I swung mightily, the edge of my hand striking the base of his skull. I made his head pitch upward and thump the seat board in front; I made his teeth grate. "That ought to do," I blurted.

Godey walled his eyes and clenched his jaws. He began to gasp and strain and flounder. His arms lifted, clawing the air. Tight as we were wedged the seat would barely hold him. Mal was ready to back up a sham and he chortled, "Look, you good people, if you want to see a feller croak." None bothered to glance.

Then Mal and me noticed the odd twist of Godey's neck. We saw his lips whiten, his ears turn tallow. His tongue waggled to speak and could not. And of a sudden we knew and sat frozen. We sat like posts while he heaved and pitched and his soles rattled the floor and his knees banged the forward seat. He bucked like a spoiled nag. . . . He quieted presently. His arms fell, his hands crumpled. He slumped and his gullet rattled.

We rode on. The mountain fell aside and the curves straightened. The highway ran a beeline. We crossed the last bridge and drew into Roscoe, halting in the square. Dee Buck stood at the door while the passengers alighted and all hastened except Old Liz and us. Old Liz ordered over her shoulder, "Go on ahead. I'll not trust a set of jaspers coming behind me." We didn't move. She whirled and her eyes lit on Godey. She sputtered, "What's the matter with him?"

Mal opened his mouth numbly. "He's doing no good," he said.

THE NEST

Nezzie Hargis rested on a clump of broomsage and rubbed her numb hands. Her cheeks smarted and her feet had become a burden. Wind flowed with the sound of water through trees high on the ridge and the sun appeared caught in the leafless branches. Cow paths wound the slope, a puzzle of trails going nowhere. She thought, "If ever I could see a smoke or hear an ax ring, I'd know the way."

Her father had said, "Nezzie, go stay a night with your Aunt Clissa;" and Mam, the woman her father had brought to live with them after her mother went away, explained, "We'd take you along except it's your ailing grandpaw we're to visit. Young'uns get underfoot around the sick." But it had not been the wish to see her grandfather that choked her throat and dampened her eyes—it was leaving the baby. Her father had reminded, "You're over six years old, half past six by the calendar clock. Now, be a little woman." Buttoned into a linsey coat, a bonnet tied on her head, she had looked at the baby wrapped in its cocoon of quilts. She would have touched its foot had they not been lost in the bundle.

Resting on the broomsage she tried to smile, but her cheeks were too tight and her teeth chattered. She recollected once kissing the baby, her lips against its mouth, its bright face pucked. Mam had scolded, "Don't paw the child. It's onhealthy." Her father had said, "Women-folks are always slobbering. Why, smack him on the foot." She had put her chin against the baby's heel and spied between its toes. Mam had cried, "Go tend the chickens." Mam was forever crying, "Go tend the chickens." Nezzie hated grown fowls—pecking hens and flogging roosters, clucking and crowing, dirtying everywhere.

Her father had promised, "If you'll go willingly to your Aunt Clissa's, I'll bring you a pretty. Just name a thing you want, something your heart is set on." Her head had felt empty. She had not been able to think what she wanted most.

She had set off, her father calling after, "Follow the path to the cattle gap, the way we've been going. And when we're home tomorrow, I'll blow the fox horn and come fetch you." But there were many trails upon the slope. The path had divided and split again, and the route had not been found after hours of searching. Beyond the ridge the path would wind to Aunt Clissa's, the chimney rising to view, the hounds barking and hurrying to meet her, and Uncle Barlow shouting, "Hold there, Digger!" and, "Stay, Merry!" and they would not, rushing to lick her hands and face.

She thought to turn back, knowing the hearth would be cold, the doors locked. She thought of the brooder house where diddles were sheltered, and where she might creep. Still across the ridge Uncle Barlow's fireplace would be roaring, a smoke lifting. She would go to the top of the ridge and the smoke would lead her down.

She began to climb and as she mounted her fingers and toes ached the more. Briars picked at the linsey coat and tugged at the bonnet. How near the crest seemed, still ever fleeing farther. No more than half of the distance had been covered when the sun dropped behind the ridge and was gone. The cold quickened, an occasional flake of snow fell. High on the ridge the wind cried, "O-oo-o."

Getting out of breath she had to rest again. Beneath a haw where leaves were drifted she drew her coat tight about her shoulders and closed her eyes. Her father's words rang in her ears:

"Just name a thing you want. . . I'll bring you a pretty."

Her memory spun in a haste like pages off a thumb. She saw herself yesterday hiding in the brooder house to play with newly hatched diddles, the brooder warm and tight, barely fitting her, and the diddles moist from the egg, scrambling to her lap, walking her spread palms, beaks chirping, "Peep, peep." Mam's voice had intruded even there: "Nezzie! Nezzie! Crack up a piece of broken dish for the hens. They need shell makings." She had kept quiet, feeling snug and contented, and almost as happy as before her mother went away.

Nezzie opened her eyes. Down the slope she saw the cow paths fading. Too late to return home, to go meeting the dark. She spoke aloud for comfort, "I ought to be a-hurrying." The words came hoarsely out of her throat. She climbed on, and a shoe became untied. She couldn't lace it anew with fingers turned clumsy and had to let the strings flare.

And she paused, yearning to turn back. She said to herself, "Let me hear a heifer bawl or a cowbell, and I will. I'll go fast." The wind moaned bitterly, drafting from the ridge into the pasture. A spring freezing among the rocks mumbled, "Gutty, gutty, gutty." She was thirsty but couldn't find it. She discovered a rabbit's bed in a tuft of grass, a handful of pills steaming beside it. The iron ground bore no tracks.

Up and up she clambered, hands on knees, now paying the trails no mind. She came to the pasture fence and attempted to mount. Her hands could not grasp, her feet would not obey. She slipped, and where she fell she rested. She drew her skirts over her leaden feet. She shut her eyes and the warmth of the lids burned. She heard the baby say, "Gub."

The baby said, "Gub," and she smiled. She heard her father ask again, "You know what 'gub' means? Means, get a move on, you slowpokes, and feed me."

She must not tarry. Searching along the panels she found a rail out of catch and she squeezed into the hole. Her dress tore, a foot came bare. She recovered the shoe. The string was frozen stiff.

A stretch of sassafras and locust and sumac began the other side of the fence. She shielded her face with her arms and compelled her legs. Sometimes she had to crawl. Bind-vines hindered, sawbriers punished her garments. She dodged and twisted and wriggled a passage. The thicket gave onto a fairly level bench, clean as a barn lot, where the wind blew in fits and rushes. Beyond it the ground ascended steeply to the top.

Dusk lay among the trees when she reached the crest of the ridge. Bending against the wind she ran across the bit of plateau to where the ridge fell away north. No light broke the darkness below, no dog barked. And there was no path going down. She called amid the thresh of boughs:

"Aunt Clissa! Uncle Barlow! It's Nezzie."

Her voice sounded unfamiliar. She cupped her hands about her mouth: "Nezzie a-calling!" Her tongue was dry and she felt a great weariness. Her head dizzied. She leaned against a tree and stamped her icy feet. Tears threatened, but she did not weep. "Be a little woman," her father had said.

A thought stirred in her mind. She must keep moving. She must find the way while there was light enough, and quickly for the wind could not be long endured. As she hurried the narrow flat the cold found the rents in the linsey coat and pierced her bonnet. Her ears twinged, her teeth rattled together. She stopped time and again and called. The wind answered, skittering the fallen leaves and making moan the trees. Dusk thickened. Not a star showed. And presently the flat ended against a wall of rock.

How thirsty she was, how hungry. In her head she saw Aunt Clissa's table—biscuits smoking, ham fussing in grease, apple cake rising. She heard Uncle Barlow's invitation: "Battle out your faces and stick your heels under the table; keep your sleeves out of the gravy and eat till you split." Then she saw the saucer of water she had left the diddles in the brooder. Her thirst was larger than her hunger.

She cowered by the wall of rock and her knees buckled. She sank to the ground and huddled there, working at the bow of her bonnet strings. Loosening the strings she chaffed her ears. And she heard her father say:

"A master boy, this little'un is. Aye, he's going somewhere in the world, I'd bet my thumb."

Mam's sharp voice replied, "Young'uns don't climb much above their raising. He'll follow his pappy in the log woods, my opinion."

"If that be the case, when he comes sixteen I'll say, 'Here,' and reach him the broadax. He'll make chips fly bigger'n bucket lids."

"Nowadays young'uns won't tip hard work. Have to be prized out of bed mornings. He'll not differ."

"I figure he'll do better in life than hoist an ax. A master boy, smart as a wasper. Make his living and not raise a sweat. He'll amount to something, I tell you."

Nezzie glimpsed the baby, its grave eyes staring. They fetched her up. She would go and spend the night in the brooder and be home the moment of its return. And she would drink the water in the diddles' saucer. She retraced her steps, walking stiffly as upon johnny-walkers, holding her hands before her. The ground had vanished, the trees more recollected than seen. Overhead the boughs groaned in windy torment.

Yet she did not start down directly, for the pitch of the slope was too fearful. She tramped the flat, going back the way she had come, and farther still. She went calling and listening. No spark broke the gloom. The dogs were mute. She was chilled to the bone when she squatted at the edge of the flat and ventured to descend. She fell in a moment, fell and rolled as a ball rolls. A clump of bushes checked her.

From there to the bench she progressed backward like a crawdabber, lowering herself by elbows and knees, sparing her hands and feet. She traveled with many a pause to thresh her arms and legs and rub her ears. It seemed forever. When she reached the bench snow was spitting.

She plodded across the bench and it had the width of the world. She walked with eyes tight to shun the sting of snowflakes. She went on, sustained by her father's voice:

"Let this chub grow up and he'll be somebody. Old woman, you can paint yore toenails and hang'em over the banisters, for there'll be hired girls to do the work. Aye, he'll see we're tuck care of."

"He'll grow to manhood, and be gone. That's about the size of it. Nowadays . . ."

Sitting on a tuft she blew her nose upon her dress tail.

Then she eased herself upon the ground with her head downhill. She began squirming left and right, gaining a few inches at each effort. She wallowed a way through briery canes, stands of sumac, thorny locusts. She bumped against rocks. Her coat snagged, her breath came in gasps. When snow started falling in earnest she was barely aware of it. And after a long struggle she pressed upon the rail fence. She groped the length of two panels in search of a hole before her strength failed.

Crouched against the fence she drew herself small into her coat. She pulled the ruffle of her bonnet close about her neck and strove against sleep. The night must be waited out. "Tomorrow," she told herself, "Pap will blow the fox horn and come for me. He will ride me on his head as he did upon an occasion." In her mind she saw the horn above the mantelpiece, polished and brass-tipped; she saw herself perched on her father's head like a topknot.

"What, now, is Pap doing?" She fancied him sitting by the hearth in her grandfather's house. "What is Grandpaw up to?" He was stretched gaunt and pale on a feather bed, his eyes keen with tricks. Once he had made a trap of his shaky hands, and had urged, "Nez', stick a finger in and feed the squirrel." In had gone her finger and got pinched. " 'T'was the squirrel bit you," he had laughed. And seeing her grandfather she thought of his years, and she thought suddenly of the baby growing old, time perishing its cheeks, hands withering and palsying. The hateful wisdom caught at her heart and choked her throat. She clenched her jaws, trying to forget. She thought of the water in the diddles' saucer. She dozed.

"Nezzie Hargis!"

She started, eyes wide to the dark.

"I'll bring you a pretty. . . . Just name a thing you want."

She trembled and her teeth chattered. She saw herself sitting with the baby on her lap. It lay with its fair head against her breast.

"Name a thing. . . something your heart is set on."

Her memory danced. She heard her father singing to quiet the baby's fret. "Up, little horse, let's hie to mill." She roved in vision, beyond her father, beyond the baby, to one whose countenance was seen as through a mist. It was her mother's face, cherished as a good dream is cherished—she who had held her in the warm, safe nest of her arms. Nezzie slept at last, laboring in sleep toward waking.

She waked to morning and her sight reached dimly across the snow. An ax hewed somewhere, the sound coming to her ears without meaning. She lifted an arm and glimpsed the gray of her hand and the bloodless fingers; she drew herself up by the fence and nodded to free her bonnet of snow. She felt no pain, only languor and thirst. The gap was three panels distant and she hobbled toward it. She fell. Lying on the ground she crammed snow into her mouth. Then she arose and passed under the bars, hardly needing to tilt her head.

Nezzie came down the slope. She lost a shoe and walked hippity-hop, one shoe on, one shoe off. The pasture was as feathery as a pillow. A bush plucked her bonnet, snatching it away; the bush wore the bonnet on a limb. Nezzie laughed. She was laughing when the cows climbed by, heads wreathed in a fog of breath, and when a fox horn blew afar. Her drowsiness increased. It grew until it could no longer be borne. She parted a clump of broomsage and crept inside. She clasped her knees, rounding the grass with her body. It was like a rabbit's bed. It was a nest.

PATTERN OF A MAN

Salt Springs, Kentucky, May 17th

Mr. Perry Wickliff, Roaring Fork, Ky.
Sir:

I take my pen in hand to ask your support of my candidacy for jailor of Baldridge County on August 5th. I've heard you lost out in a school shuffle last year. They say you were ousted as teacher at Spring Branch in the middle of the term and have rented land off of Zeb Thornton and trying to farm. It chokes my heart to think of one with your learning digging holes and plowing balks. A schoolteacher with paper hands battling dirt!

If any county needs top scholars, it's Baldridge. I'm bound there's a politician behind the deal, and it stands to reason you're bitter as an oak gall. When elected I'll use my power in your behalf. Whoever the gentleman who frisked you out of a job, I'll have him out on a limb like a screech owl shoving a chicken.

In a jailor race any hound dog can run and candidates are thicker than yellow jackets at a stir-off. You don't have to know book letters from cow horns, or to have ever darkened a schoolhouse door. On that account a big bunch will file for office. I've underwent six years of education and I'm no dumb-head. I'll be the only candidate who can make out print bottom up—a trick I learnt reading newspaper wallpaper in boyhood. Many a deputy sheriff has scratched his head at my recital of a warrant in this fashion. I've been unlucky in the way of getting indicted for this and that and have spent more time in jail than any other innocent man in the mountains. Point a finger at me and I look guilty. Yet I've kept my name clear. Nothing ever stuck on me.

Before the election ends you'll hear lies, candidates smutting each other's reputations. They'll wear the hollows out slick rooting for votes. O you can't run a race without getting banged. The strongest they'll hit the hardest. Already they're spreading a tale about me and a gum of bees. I ask Justice, Can I rule what bees will do? I sold a gum to a neighbor and nine days later the critters came swarming home.

On account of the contrariness of bee nature I suffered a month's confinement in the Crossbar Hotel. That's what the jaspers on the inside call it. I ate victuals Lazarus would of culled, slept on a mattress jake-walking with chinch bugs. And fleas! The cracks were hopping with them. As we'd say, if the flats don't bite you the sharps will. And hear me. Floors and walls begged for lye soap and shuck mops. The grub was so rough we used to swear you had to wear gloves to eat it. And that's where I struck my notion.

I struck on a notion to become the jailor. I swore to

myself I would run for it next go-round, and when I'd nailed the job down, to bring my woman and live in the jailhouse. My woman would keep the place as clean as snow. Where my doughbeater has a hand you'll not find a speck of dust big enough to put in your eye. And we would feed meals a man could enjoy picking his teeth after. Chicken and dumplings every Sunday. A county lock-up needs a woman's fussing, and a woman's hate of gom.

I crave your vote and influence, for I hear you're well thought of over there. Canvas the Roaring Fork people in my behalf and I'll pull ropes to win you back a school job. Once I knew Roaring as I know my *a-b-ab's*, and many the woman will recollect me and my rounding ways. It happens I've not set foot in the section for a couple of years. But I found my wife on Fern Branch, a prong of Roaring, and I'm married-kin to a plenty of folks in your territory.

Now, listen to me. While canvassing you might see a girl fair to the eye who can be talked into matrimony. I hear you live by your lorn self. Twenty-six years old and not wed! What in thunder! Can you stand to eat your own cooking?

Till I get there myself to clap the hands of the voters, begin swinging them in my favor. I stand well in the opinion of all, except Zeb Thornton—a tough one to deal with, as you may have discovered. A hard number, that Zeb.

It's my aim to travel the length of Roaring Fork, up every draw and trace and hollow. First my pieded pony must be shod before she walks the rocks, and I'm waiting to see who and how many join the race. The county court clerk says sixteen have filed and a big lot are on the borders of it. The more candidates, say I, the better.

I lay down my pen.

Crafton Rowan

Salt Springs, Ky, May 28th

Dear Perry Wickliff:

I've been plaguing the mail rider ten days. After the trouble I took writing to you I feel a reply is my right. Has a body spoken against me, or are you busy trying to raise a crop? A farming life is contrary to education. Why, I bet you don't know what makes a pig's tail curl. And you may be one of these sharp tacks who scorn to plant by the almanac. Being Zeb Thornton owns the land, I'm bound he has put his worst off on you. Land so clayey you can hear corn sprouting at thirty yards. Did my pony have shoes, I'd trot over and see how you fare.

Now, before Zeb Thornton poisons your mind against me I'll tell you the law trouble we had three years ago. Zeb, to my shape of thinking, is a form of cattle buyer it pays to have few dealings with. Mealymouthed, two-faced, slick as a dogwood hoe handle. That's Zeb all over.

56

I had a heifer growing into a cow, nubbins of horns blossoming, petted nigh to death. My woman had set stake on keeping her for milk and butter. Comes Zeb knocking at the door of a winter evening, trailed by a drove of cattle. I welcomed him under my roof as I would any of God's creations, and I fed and quartered his stock. Next morning he spied my heifer and took advantage of being company. He wore my mind down bargaining and paid me eight dollars. Cold robbery, if ever I named it, and my woman came within a pea of leaving me.

Zeb mixed my calf amongst his brutes and went herding down-creek, acting like the king of the pen-hookers. But my heifer had a will of her own. She stole away and hid in my barn. The next shot out of the barrel Zeb arrived with a deputy sheriff, bearing a warrant. Nine days I suffered the lock-up before making bail, although I later proved my innocence in court. Was Zeb Thornton the last man earthly, I wouldn't do another lick of trading with him.

Twenty-one candidates have filed in the jailor race and a rumor goes a wad more are ready to jump in. There's even a woman on the ticket, with about as much chance as a snowball in Torment. She's as pretty a fixing as I ever saw, but that won't help her at the polls. In my time Baldridge County won't vote itself under a petticoat government. I say, let as many as wants pitch in their hats, be they hens or roosters, boars or sows.

They'll split the vote more directions than a turkey's foot. They'll whittle their following to a nub.

All the main creeks have one candidate at least, except Roaring. Roaring Fork is virgin territory. Broad Creek has five, Grassy Branch three. Big Ballard has nine. Others here and there. I'm counting to go solid around Salt Spring as I'm kin to everybody and his pappy, kin through my wife. And in spite of Garlan Hurley who has filed against me. My opinion, he'll get two votes, his own and his woman's. Beyond that he won't stain paper. And I ought to run well on Roaring due to my wife. Aye, could I stack Roaring's votes on top of Salt Springs I'd be as good as elected. For once I'd go into jail by law and right, the key in my hand.

Work for my election and I'll have you principal of a school even if it croaks every politician in the county. I'll have you teaching young'uns quicker than hell can singe a feather. It smothers my heart to know hard learning is being dragged along a furrow, wasting to moles and crows. My old teacher used to say that once a body breathed chalk dust and pounded the Big Thick Dictionary he was spoiled for common labor. Name the schoolhouse you would be master of. I'll ring you.

Hear me. I'll be coming to Roaring Fork the minute I find shoes to fit my nag. She's finicky as a woman and won't travel barefooted.

Keep your eyes skinned for a wife.

Faithfully,

Crafton

Perry Wickliff:

I've got wits that beat seven indictments, I've had lawyers walking on pencils, but danged my eyes if I can make sense of why you answered my letter by word of mouth. I've been of the belief mail carriers were paid to haul messages in envelopes, not in their skulls. How much postage did you stick on his upper lip?

How big the yarn swelled in the carrier's head is on-telling. When a tale passes teeth twice you won't recognize it. Anyhow, what he told I wouldn't have had made public for a war pension. I figure it has cost me in the neighborhood of a dozen votes. The gist of it was I had attempted to bribe you into working for my election—a falsehood and you know it. I asked you free will, no strings tied.

My burden in life to be misjudged. I aimed to help you stop farming, a trade you couldn't master to the day you die. I get my jowls slapped. Worry you not, I'll win the race beholden to none, fair field and no favor. Of the thirty-two candidates at this writing I'm the only one with the policy of moving into the jailhouse stick, stove, bed and wife. I'm the pattern of a man who understands what a lock-up needs. From cold experience I know the head-down feet-up way it's now being operated. They don't know dirt from horse manure.

At last Roaring Fork has a candidate, some jasper who calls himself Muldraugh. My opinion, a stalking horse put in by Zeb Thornton to snag my votes. Like the female candidate, he hasn't an icicle's chance in a hot skillet. Muldraugh, aye. What kind of a name is that? He was born yon side Pound Gap, in Virginia, a full sixty-five miles from here, and didn't move into our country until he was a right smart sized boy. The day hasn't come when this county will support a foreigner for public office.

Perry Wickliff, if you still want to climb on my band-wagon, I've left the tailgate down. Yet mount of your own accord. I'll plague you no longer for scattering your brains to the sparrows and living in a bachelor's hell. A final offer I make. Would you take the school at Dirk, a hop and jump from your scarecrow farm? Whoever is the teacher, I'll have him flagged out.

Forty-three candidates had filed by the day they closed the books. So many running the winner won't need more than a double handful of votes. I figure I'll win by a basket full.

Faithfully,

Crafton Rowan

Salt Springs, June 8th

You, there, Perry Wickliff:

I got the post card and have sized you up as a fellow with no more political sense than a dry-land goose. Are you too stingy to paste a stamp on a letter? Why, mail carriers spend half the day reading post cards and spreading the news. So you advise me to hurry shoes on my spoiled nag and come speak for myself. And you hint Roaring Fork hasn't seen my face in forever. This coming from a man who beyond a doubt was rode out of a schoolhouse on a rail.

My opinion, you've fallen into Zeb Thornton's trap head and ears. The reason I haven't been over for a spell is a personal matter not a whit ruled by the oath Zeb swore at the time of our calf trouble, his threatening my life did I so much as set a toe in the Roaring valley. A free country. I'll travel anywhere I get a ripe notion, and if I choose to shun a mother-in-law's district to keep the family peace, that's my right too. I vow I've had my last trade and traffic with Zeb Thornton.

On behalf of my pieded pony, I'll say she's less spoiled than the common run of folks. Has more sense than a tub of educated fools playing farmer. She can do every-thing but talk, and so gentle you can sit in a chair and curry her. She's bare-hoofed as a tenderfooted critter ought to be until her true size is located. If it comes to a force put, I'll forge a pair of shoes for her my own self.

Wickliff, I'm seeking the full facts of why you were cut loose from that teaching job. I smell a rat hide. Upon my word and honor, it appears the political foxes of Baldridge County done a good deed for once. They got rid of a sorry schoolmaster.

I'd stake my hat the crows are starving in your fields.
Crafton Rowan

Dear Perry:

During the past month you have caused me trouble and sorrow beyond my human due. After the varmity manner you treated my jail race I sunk so low in spirit I let Garlan Hurley talk me out of running for the office. He figured to heir my Salt Spring votes. He wore me down into accepting forty-five dollars. But ho! Before I could get to the clerk's office to withdraw, my name had been sent to the printers. My name was on paper.

Could I lie down on a legal ballot? It was run whether or no. No two ways talking. I had to repay Garlan or stand up to bullets. But I'd already been fleeced of the money. The son of a gun who owns the land adjoining mine claimed I'd swung over on his side and cut timber. I ask, Who knows where lines run nowadays with the landmarks gone, the streams changed course? Any jury would have handed in a verdict in my favor. Yet you can't fight law battles while running races. My neighbor got my forty-five dollars, Garlan Hurley my pieded pony.

Are you a fellow who will acknowledge an honest debt? Recollect the message you sent by the mail carrier early in June, and the postcard shortly thereafter? By my soul, they cost me at least thirty-six votes. I'm of a mind there are three dozen uncommitted you could swing to me. A word said in my behalf would drop them into my pocket—enough with Salt Springs' backing to ring me in. I'm counting on you to settle your obligation.

With crops layed-by it would do you pleasant to travel the waters of Roaring head to mouth. You stir out little, goes the talk. Folks rarely see a hair of you. That's not right, living like you do. Marry, say I. Any good woman will do. Marry and start filling up the house with babies. Then you'll have something to live and work for.

Listen to me, Perry. Old Stedam Byrd, a mile down-creek, has two single daughters, twenty years old or so. Big, hefty girls, not yet claimed. Spruce up your horse, angle your hat, and go visit them Sunday. Begin lining things up for yourself and my candidacy. They'll pour the fried chicken to you, with a horn of something to drink beforehand to make it slick down easy. Stedam controls four votes.

I've come on the true reason you left that teaching job in the middle of the school term. A trustee reports you waked him at midnight to say that after six years of teaching you were bone-tired of minding other people's young'uns. I declare you justified, remembering when a chunk of a boy I ran teachers distracted. Why, I struck a match once that burnt a schoolhouse down.

The reports lately claim your cornfields are the blackest and the growingest in the mountains, due to the extra seasoning of rain Roaring Fork alone enjoyed this year.

Faithfully,

Crafton

Dear Perry:

I would travel to Roaring and start canvassing if I had a beast to ride, and if I didn't have to keep a lookout here. With candidates thicker than horseflies at a stock sale, I daren't take eyes off my voters. Garlan Hurley and others of his sorry pattern are trying to wean the loyalty of my blood kin. Who Garlan's kin is, don't ask. He couldn't name his own pappy.

What hurts, these jaspers are imping my policy, declaring for a clean jail and home cooking. Trying to cut my throat with my own butcher knife.

I believe to my heart Garlan's another stalking horse put in by somebody. Everything's in a rigamaroar. A misery to win a vote and then have to turn sheep dog and guard it against thieves. Bat an eye and you've lost lambs.

My faith in humankind tells me you are working in my behalf. Let it out about the candidate on your creek being a foreigner, not of this country. And don't forget Ben Manley's influence—the Ben at the mouth of Buckeye Branch. I've learnt he has two daughters pretty enough to draw skims across a male's sight. I recollect their mother, a picture-piece at sixteen with catbird's eggs for eyes. And she'll remember me, though won't admit it. I recollect she plaited her hair into two big plaits. I'd take and tie'em together, and latch them under my chin. Aye, the good old days! Ben Manley votes three.

O I miss my pieded pony as I would my feet. I've walked until my ham-strings are rebelling.

Faithfully,

Crafton

Salt Springs, July 30th

Perry:

Seven days until the election. Time's burning. Hurry along to Moab Colley's place on Oak Trace. One daughter left untaken in his household. She's not a pullet, has shed her pin feathers, but bear in head you're on the high side of the twenties. The thing is, Moab gives his daughters fifty dollars, a cow, a walnut bedstead and nine quilts to start them in life. He votes five.

The way the signs are reading the old jailor can prepare himself to clap the big key into my hand come the first of the year. With forty-three candidates tearing up the patch a small wad of votes will fan a body in. Aye, my election is safe as gold. My solid Salt Springs following, stacked onto the votes tricked from under the whiskers of candidates elsewheres, and laid alongside the Roaring Fork support, ought to raise a pile nobody can top. When they open the ballot boxes—heepee! Watch the geese fly out.

The master crop of corn you've raised is the wonder

of the county. A rumor says it might run to sixty-five bushels to the hillside acre. In this world the Man Above throws a mighty weight to the side of those who know not what they are doing.

Faithfully,

Crafton

Salt Springs, August 4th

Perry:

I hasten this postcard, the only rag of paper in the house. A last favor I ask. Go to the polls tomorrow, stand as close to the ballot box as the law allows, and a span closer, and urge the folks to pile on a winner. Say I'm the pattern of a man to elect.

I figure I've got the jail job in the frog of my hand. Hurrah for me!

Craft

BALDRIDGE COUNTY JAIL

August 11th

Dear Perry:

I've borrowed this sheet of paper off the jailor to let you hear my side of the case against me. I ask Justice, Can I rule what a spoiled pony will do? Can a body legally be jailed for giving a critter food and shelter when it turns up hungry and barefooted at his barn gate? Garlan Hurley kept her a solid month and never bothered to nail shoes to her tender feet. O he's not got a heart, just a big wart in his chest. But I can read this case bottomside up. I'll come clear in court. Nothing ever stuck on me.

Perry, I'm trying to raise bail. And the only cattle trader I know of who will buy calves off-season is Zeb Thornton. Let out to him I have a couple of fine heifers, both promising milk and butter makers. And he's to deal through me, and not let my wife know. It's a force put.

I can't groan for laughing at the way a female beat out a raft of men in the jailor's race. Thrashed us to a fare-ye-well. Every man jack of us had to go to the bull-hole. She rounded up more votes than the rest of us put together. Yet I don't understand it. All signs seem to fail nowadays.

I'll be here when the woman takes office in January unless I can sell my calves and make bail, and unless the chinch bugs walk off with me plumb. Always I've claimed the county lock-up needs a woman's broom and skillet—a woman with a man standing by. On your behalf I want to report she is fair as a picture, and single.

Faithfully,

Crafton Rowan

MAYBIRD UPSHAW

To THE day I perish I will recollect Maybird Upshaw being hauled into my yard on Shepherds Creek in a wagon. She was my wife's kin, widowed by her second husband's death at the mines; she was the largest woman ever I set eyes upon.

The threshold creaked as Maybird pushed into the house. She sat on a trunk as we had no chair of a size to hold her. She dwarfed my wife and made a mouse of the baby. I recollect she sighed, "I've come to visit a while," and breathed deep with satisfaction. "I aim to rest me a spell."

"You're welcome if you can live hardscrabble," said Trulla, fastening cold eyes on me, eyes blue as gun-metal. I knew she was thinking Maybird might be on our hands for life.

"We have only old-fashioned comforts," I spoke, brushing a hand behind my ears for I stood in mortal need of a haircut. My eyes roved the log walls, coming to rest on Maybird, her large fair head with tresses rich as fire, the drapes of flesh hanging her arms, knees dimpled as the baby's cheeks. I tried to figure her weight. She was as big as a salt barrel. She had the world beat.

A smile caught Maybird's face. "I'm not picky," she declared, "and anywhere's better than a coal camp." She made a book of her hands. "I'll stop off here a while, then be moving on. I don't intend to burden."

"You'll miss the camps," I reminded, feeling Trulla's stare boring my skull. "Credit at the commissary when you're of a notion to buy, green money on pay day, picture shows and circuses. They say when you've breathed gob smoke you're ruined for country air. And Shepherds Creek is as lorn a place as a body can discover."

"I'm not of a mind to stay long in any single spot," Maybird said. "I can't live content in a valley for wondering what's yonder side of the mountain. Ah, I've lived in a lot of camps—Blue Cannel, Hardblock, Alicecoal, Oxeye. And if I had my rathers, I'd not stick my feet more than once under any table. During the days of my life I aim to see the whole of creation."

"A widow-woman would starve," Trulla argued, "traveling here and yon."

Maybird's face lit. Gold freckles shone on her nose. "My mother taught me to make wax blossoms when a child, window bouquets, mantel dressing and funeral wreaths. Why, I'll earn my way selling false flowers. The Turks-cap lilies and roses I pattern would fool butterflies. One sight of a blossom and I can shape a match to it."

"I've never yearned to travel," Trulla said, snatching up the baby and jouncing it nervously. "My longing

69

is for a house with high ceilings and tall windows. But here stands the log pen of a homeseat I married. I'm tied to a man who is satisfied to live the same as his grandsire."

I let pass Trulla's complaint, being proud of the old-timey log dwelling which had been in the family more than a hundred years; I kept feasting my eyes on Maybird, and rousing courage to ask her weight.

"It's not my notion to settle down," Maybird went on. "I weary of viewing the same things over and over. Soon I'll be wandering along."

"While you're relaxing," Trulla suggested, "you might begin to make false flowers. We'll rob our bee gums and have wax in plenty."

Maybird chuckled. "Then I can start laying-by for my rambling." She began to laugh. Joy rose in her as cream to the lip of a milk jar. "Only would somebody peddle my bouquets at the camps. Thirty-five cents they ought to bring, fifty if the mines are working double shifts."

Trulla's face sharpened. "My man can go sell the flowers. He needs mightily to discover a barber anyhow. He has played Sampson long enough."

I squirmed. "A man drumming flowers? To sell firewood, or corn, or garden sass, I'd not mind. But peddling wax would be bitter hard. It's not man's work."

Maybird stirred and the hinges of the trunk rasped. She lifted a huge hand. "Just say they're Maybird

Upshaw's pattern. Summer blooms for dresser tops. Blossoms to brighten a table, never to fade. They'll remember. O, I'd go myself if I could get about handy." She cast a spiteful glance at the narrow door.

I hummed and hawed, and finally to change the talk I plucked courage and asked, "Maybird, how much do you weigh?" I didn't want to hear more about flower peddling. And if Trulla's quick look had been a blade my throat would have been cut.

But Maybird was proud of her size. She tossed her great head. "The day I was born," she said, "I tipped the scales at three pounds and a quarter—so tiny I was bedded on a pillow. At eighteen I weighed two hundred and eighty-five on the steelyards, yet for the past six years I've had no way to learn. The checkweighman's scales at the mines won't register under a thousand. My opinion, I'm safe to weigh four hundred."

"Your weight might hinder travel," Trulla remarked sharply.

"Now, no," Maybird declared, "I'll go the world around. In Kentucky I aim to see where the Frenches and the Eversoles fit their feud, and the Hatfields and the McCoys. I'll look on Natural Bridge and the Breaks of the Big Sandy River. I'll see Abe Linkhorn's birthplace, and where a battle was fit at Perryville. And I've heard afar west the fires of Torment spout from the ground, and the devil's boiling kettle throws up a steam. I'll see what there is to see."

"You ought to of been a gypsy," I said, "living in a cloth house, reading hands for bread, traipsing place to place."

Maybird laughed softly. She blushed the mad color of her hair.

I walked to Oxeye mine camp the hottest September day in memory; and I felt like a dunce carrying a mess of false flowers. But Trulla's one fixed thought was to make certain of Maybird's departure before she grew too heavy ever to move again. Already it was tuggety-pull to get her through any door.

I knocked at the first house and I was as scared as the day I married. I brushed my hair under the back brim of my hat. Waiting, I spied about. Camp houses marched the hills and gob smoke fed into the sky. Babies were crying. Everywhere hung the smell of soot and dish-water.

A beardy fellow cracked the door, his woman crowd-ing behind him. I lifted a bouquet. "Maybird Upshaw—" I began, and my throat frogged.

"Big May?" he asked.

His wife snatched the blossoms. "One thing about the large," she said, "they have good hearts. Generous, gee-o! Maybird always gave us flowers. We were neighbors. Thank Maybird. Thanks."

The door slammed and I was not a chip the richer.

A miner came along, his cap lamp burning in broad

daylight. I inquired, "Are there double shifts working these days?"

"Yis." He stared as if he had met a witty. "Are you drumming them flowers?" I was holding a bunch as you might a dead cat by the tail.

I dipped my head.

"A carnival has pitched at the ballground and folks won't spend a dime elsewheres. Oxeye Camp has gone show-crazy."

I knocked on many a door, not selling a blossom. "For sale?" they would say. "That doesn't sound like Maybird. She used to give us a vase full. To my knowledge she never sold a petal. She was that freehearted." Or, "I've only the price of the carnival, else I'd buy." An old-faced child said, "Maybird is the biggest show ever I seed. The awfulest foot! I bet she weighs a jillion." And she stared at the hair escaping my hat.

In mid-afternoon a woman called after me. She bought a bouquet and paid two dimes and a nickel. "I'll pitch in to help a widow-woman good days or bad," she said. "Anyhow, nobody but Maybird can pattern flowers so really-like." And then I heard music afar and saw tents on the ballground, and a mighty wheel turning, and with lights ringing it. People hurried by, and I followed.

The carnival folk yawned in the sun, blinking like owls. A music engine played. A weight-guesser held his hat in the crook of an elbow and shouted among a thicket of walkingsticks: "I come within three pounds!

Your weight within three! A gentleman's cane if I fail."
Miners and their women and children shucked out money to see MAN OR BEAST? and MARVELS OF AMERICA.

I held the flowers behind me, and I asked the guesser a question. "Can you figure a woman's weight, sight unseen?"

He spoke swiftly, "If I'm given an idea of her measurements."

"I'll pay a quarter."

"Hand over. Right-tow. How tall? Broad of beam? Size of shoe?"

I told the best I could. I spread my arms, holding forth the flowers, though I couldn't circle so great a space as Maybird covered. I took a walkingstick and drew on the ground. "She's so stout she looks notable," said I.

The weight-guesser blew between his teeth. "She's a whale," he cried. "Gaffney ought to hear about her."

"It's my belief she's a finer view than any you have here," I bragged.

He jerked an elbow toward MARVELS OF AMERICA.

"We have a dame weighing four hundred and twenty, but no match to the madam you've reported." He clapped the quarter back into my hand, and a ticket beside, and told me to see the show tee-total. "And take a gander at Mary Mammoth," he said. He didn't try to guess Maybird's weight.

"I ought to be going," I said, but I stayed to watch the acting dogs. I saw a fool swallow a sword; a lack-brain ate fire balls; a human creature reposed on a bed of spikes. I saw Mary Mammoth sitting on a platform, eating a meal. She nibbled a dish of lettuce leaves and drank from a nail hole in a can. Compared to Maybird she looked puny.

The weight-guesser called me over when I quit the tent. "Shake hands with Gaffney, the boss," he said. And Gaffney asked, "What's your opinion of Mary?"

"She'll do in a pinch," I said, and I felt a wax petal strike my shoe. The flowers were melting in the heat. "But my wife's sister-in-law dwarfs all womankind— firm-fleshed, plump cheeks, the picture of life. More pounds to her statue than ever I saw a human pack. Why, it took a two-horse wagon to haul her to Shepherds Creek."

Gaffney lifted an arm. "The lady belongs in a side show. She'd draw customers like honey draws flies."

"My belief," I agreed.

Maybird kept gaining weight. And was she an eater! She could stash away a peck at a sitting. She stripped the garden, emptied the meatbox. People came to look at her, and they ate also. I ran up a store debt. And I got joshed. A wag at the post-office said, "I hear there's going to be a trial in the magistrate's court next Saturday." I bit, "What over?" Laughed he, "To try and see if Big May can sit in a number two washtub." The joke was on him. Even a number four tub would have been tight squeezing.

You could nearly see Maybird gaining. Before Gaffney came it got to where she couldn't pass through the door. We tugged and pulled, shoved and pushed, to no success. Trulla wanted me to widen the opening but I vowed it would destroy the house pattern. You mustn't fiddle with a butt-notched log dwelling. The building would have to be torn down ridgepole to sleepers to deliver Maybird. She was as trapped as a fox in a hen coop.

Trulla worried and grew cross. She would moan to me, "Of what use for the head of the carnival to come now that Maybird's prisoned inside." And Trulla turned hard to live with. The least thing and she took the rag off the bush. I couldn't glance at Maybird, much less carry on a conversation with her, without Trulla flying off the hinges. Never could I figure a woman's mind. Once she got the fidgets and took a notion to cut my hair. I stood in uncommon need of a trimming. But I saw the metal in her eyes, her chin trembling. I inched away, scared to have her near me with anything sharp in hand.

The carnival people came on a Thursday. I was in the barn, spying into a piece of looking glass, trying to crop my temples with mule shears. I heard hoofs rattle rocks, a singing of wheels, and a voice cry, "Whoa-ho!"

I hustled across the lot and sprang over the fence. A wagon and team stood in the yard. I heard Gaffney and the weight-guesser talking to Maybird inside the house. Maybird was sighing, "I'm held here everlastingly. I can't get out." Gaffney answered, "I didn't wrestle ferris wheels and cyclodromes thirty years for nothing. A way will be devised." The weight-guesser nodded.

I went in to bid the visitors welcome and offer chairs. Trulla stood back, shut-mouthed, too timid before strangers to practice manners. The first chance I whispered to the weight-guesser, "How much do you figure Maybird will pull on the scales?"

The weight-guesser calculated, one eye squinted to sharpen his view; he dug fingers into his scalp. "Five hundred and seven," he blurted, "and I've not missed three pounds."

Gaffney snapped his fingers with satisfaction. "We'll bill her as THE WORLDLY WONDER," he said. And directly he set about inspecting the butt-locked logs of the front wall. He surveyed inside and out.

I was uneasy. I said, "Could we get a block and tackle, we might lift her up through the roof. No harm done to tear off a few shakes."

"Ah, no," he said. "Twisting the wrist is my calling. And all I'll need is a crowbar and a hammer." With a hammer's claws he pried loose the door facing and set it aside. The logs to the height of the door were left supported only at the corner.

I swallowed air. My Adam's apple jerked. I was in misery.

"We'll not damage," he said, and he and the weight-guesser worked the bar between the bottom log and the sleepers and prized up and forward.

I expected the worse. My breath caught.

The walls budged. Five logs raised in their notches and swung gate-fashion. The house opened like a turkey crate. A passage was made and Maybird walked through. Then the logs were jimmied back into place and the facing restored.

We hoisted Maybird into the wagon. She sat on the wagonbed and laughed, her face bright as a wax blossom, her hair wealthy as the sun.

Gaffney and the weight-guesser climbed onto the spring seat, and they rode away. And Trulla began to cry. She clapped a hand on my shoulder and her eyes had the glint of new nails. She got me into the house, found scissors and worked me over. She whacked and gapped. She nearly ran out of hair. She skinned me alive.

THE SHARP TACK

Standing Rock, Kentucky
March 2, 1946

Mr. Talt Evarts
Wiley, Ky.

Dear Mr. Evarts:

I wouldn't know you from Adam's off-ox, and I'm not the pattern of a man to butt into the affairs of others. Say I, Let every man-jack attend to his own affairs, and stay out of the shade of the next fellow. What's not a body's business, play deaf and dumb to it. But lately strange tales have been drifting from Wiley Town, lies strong enough to melt the wax in a body's ears. They concern the Man Above, and what concerns Him concerns me. As His disciple, whoever steps on His toes mashes mine.

For half of a lifetime I've preached amongst the hills and hollows of Baldridge County. I've served more folks than you have reckoning of. Married them, buried them, and tried to save their souls betwixt and between. There isn't a churchhouse or oak bower in Baldridge County in which I haven't trod the pulpit and preached the Book. It's my burden on earth to be watchdog to the sheep, unfrocker of the wolf wearing the lamb's clothing, scourger of the wicked. Well, sir, I'm writing to you on your behalf. I take my pen in hand to say that you are within singeing distance of hellfire and eternal damnation.

Our soldier boys have come home telling a mixture of things. Most handle only the truth and if wonders they viewed grow a mite big in their mouths I lay it to high spirits. Didn't they fit the good fight across the waters, risk their necks to slay the heathen? Didn't they send money home? To their reports I'm all ears. I grunt and I say "O!" and, "Ah!" A grandson of mine climbed a tower in Italy called Pisa, and to hear him tell it it was out of whanker, leaning on air, against nature and the plan of the Almighty. Plumb si-goggling! An anticky falsehood, I figure. Trying to see how big he could blow the pig's bladder before it busts. But your tale— yours is humbug of a different character. I've had it direct you've returned bearing a mortal untruth. And some are believing it. To learn of it jarred my heart.

People inform me you are claiming to have been to the Holy Land. They say you've brought a cedar sprout from Lebanon where King Solomon cut his temple timber and aim to plant it in Baldridge County soil. Upon my word and deed and honor! This cross-grains my fifty-one years of ministry in His Name. It sets to naught my long and weary labors.

Now, listen, mister boy. I'm a Bible worm. I've read it lid to lid. I testify only the dead and the saved ever journey to that Country—those risen from the grave, and that's not to be until Resurrection Day. The Holy Land is yonder in the sky and there's no road to it save by death and salvation. The fashion you spout lies, any minute I expect to hear of you passing through Jericho on an ass and visiting Zion. As for the cedar bush, where you hooked it is not where you claim. Our hills and hollows have as much need for it as a boar has for tits. Jump on it. Tramp it into the ground.

I have a sermon which fits you like bark fits a tree. But it would use up a horn of ink to pen it. Besides, writing it I'd have to leave off the singing. My text would be on sharp tacks who twist Scripture to confound people and abet the Serpent. For one particular, they declare the world is round as a mushmelon, while the Book says plainly it has four corners. They start new congregations to peddle their corkscrew religion. They can quote you chapter and verse, aye-o, but they bear no fruit. They preach, and Old Horny reaps the benefit. I say, There's just one sect—the True Church. The rest are insects.

My advice to you is to hush your wild talk and line up behind common sense. You're riding a horse with the blind staggers. Saddle a fresh mount, say I. If you're bound to foam at the mouth, tell of seeing twenty-foot snakes as a soldier boy hereabouts vows he saw in Africa. Or of a people with lips the size of saucers. Or of a tombstone in the land of Egypt covering thirteen acres. Tall stories of that sort are evil, yet not fatal to the soul. Hark my counsel, or you're going as straight to hell as a martin to its gourd. And hell is not a haystack.

Jerb Powell

Standing Rock
March Eleventh

Talt Evarts
Wiley, Ky.

Let you open your mouth and out jumps a toad-frog. What further demon-gotten claims are to leap forth? The news comes you are now showing a chunk of marble you say was dug from King Solomon's quarry under the city of Jerusalem. Dug where Old Sol got his building rock for the Temple's foundations. Great balls of thunder! Can't you learn to separate heaven from earth?

Why didn't you follow the pattern of other soldier boys and bring home fighting knives and German guns and Jape swords? There are enough brought-on weapons in and about Standing Rock to wage a battle. Aye gonnies, the Silver War might of come out different did our side have them then. You should have latched on to honest relics. Cephus Harbin's Rufus has a chip off the rock of Gibraltar. A couple more wars and Gibraltar won't be of a size to strike a match on. My grandnephew sports a watch charm made from a toe he knocked off of a statue in France. Yet you couldn't be satisfied unless you fetched something fiendish. Hasn't a bloody war contented your mind? What else will it take to satisfy your lust for chicanery?

Your falsehoods are spreading like the Spanish grippe and some dumb-heads are believing them. It appears you could paint goose manure and sell it for gold. You've already caused me two run-ins. Our plug of a postmaster said I ought to crawl out of my terrapin shell and join the universe. Said I hadn't done my "home work"—whatever that means. I fixed the jasper. Told him did he swap brains with a jaybird it would fly backward. And I've tilted with our ignorant schoolteacher. He's a round-earth believer. O they're scratching under rocks to find schoolmasters nowadays.

The teacher started it. Said, "Reckon you've heard about the soldier boy from Wiley visiting the Holy Land." Says I, "I've heard the world is the shape of a crab apple, but that's not speaking I'm believing it. It's contrary to the Teachings. If I swallow that I'll have to agree water runs uphill and Chinamen walk with their heads hanging." He insisted, "The boy was on the very spot. No two ways talking." Spake I, "A host of the righteous will rise from the grave on Judgment Day and fly there. None now treading the earth has passed through the gates of pearl and returned to tattle about it." You ought to of seen his countenance when I wised him up. His jaws sagged like a gate.

In olden times Noah sent a bird flying the waters. He sent a dove on particular business. But hey! Who sent you? Old Scratch? Lucifer incarnate? Old Gouge? The Book speaks of the behemoth. Why didn't you snatch a behemoth whisker? And I ask, Has any other traveler matched your claim of visiting Up Yonder? Now, no. A thousand counts no.

I'm not scorning the miracles of the age. Some truths are evident, known without witnessing. Joab Gipson's eldest son flew over Germany and dropped bombs down the throats of the enemy. Roan Thomas's son bore no gun in the fray. He fit with balls of fire spouted from a nozzle. Dial Roberts was an underwater sailor, traveled the bowels of the seas in a vessel. I fling my hat to the boys who punished the followers of the crooked cross.

Harken. Cease your blasphemy. Quit *baaing* on the order of a broken-mouth ram. Destroy the cedar sprout as you would a copperhead snake. And hey! A chunk of marble makes the best sort of hone to sharpen razors.

Jerb Powell

March Twenty-first

Talt Evarts:

A dunce I was to even mention a behemoth. I hear you are declaring them hippopotamuses, critters that live somewhere on this earth. Hell's bangers! Are you in cahoots with Beelzebub? Aye, your tongue is a viper which continues to wiggle even after its head is cut off. I'm here to announce you are shoving yourself into a picklement. When you die, my opinion, there won't be a preacher worthy of the name willing to hold a service over your carcass.

A thought keeps itching my mind. While you were soldiering how did you manage to traipse all over the map. Why weren't you busy pumping bullets into the gizzards of the adversary? Throughout the war I had my ear glued to the news. As I recollect, no armies shot lead mines at each other in a country called Holy Land. Wheresoever it was you journeyed, did you sneak away to it from the battle? Upon my honor, I believe you white-eyed.

I'm a preacher, bear in head. The promise of Hereafter is a rapture to my heart, reckless tidings such as you bear a pain and a sorrow. Had I half a suspicion you had been to the real On High, a yoke of oxen couldn't of held me here at Standing Rock. To Wiley Town I would have hied. On hands and knees if necessary. Crawled if no other way. A peck of questions I would of asked: How wide the streets of gold? How sounded the trumpets of Tomorrow? How fared the blessed where ten thousand years is but a day? Being in my right mind, I stayed at home. Naturally. I wasn't born yesterday.

Talt Evarts, I've strove earnestly with you. I've written you letters you never answered, licked stamps and wasted paper trying to purge your stony heart. To no profit. You're buckled to the Devil. I've cut out toeholds for you on the down-road, still you insist on sliding toward perdition. The time is short. My patience has worn thin as a dime. I won't struggle with you eternally.

Jerb Powell

April Second

Mr. Talt Evarts:

I would have bet my thumbs I'd not again black paper in your behalf. I had capped the ink bottle. But I've met with something which puts a different cast on matters. It came out of another argument with the Standing Rock teacher. I learnt a speck. I'll admit it. Aye, I aim to keep learning till my toes turn up. The teacher stayed mired in his own folly while I began to spy a ray of daylight. The teacher—you might know him. I won't handle his name. I wouldn't want to dirty my tongue.

Well, sir, this jasper pulls a geography on me. He opened her up to a map where a dot stood for Jerusalem, a dot for Tiberius, a patch for the Dead Sea, a streak for the river Jordan. Printed up plain as my nose. For the split of a second I was stumped. What were these precious names doing in a book taught scholars at the tender age? Had the sharp tacks been at work? Then wisdom struck. It knocked me like the bolt which hit Paul on the Damascus Road. The whole thing came as clear as a baby's eye. I said, "Anybody two inches wide between the ears ought to be able to figure how these names got into a geography. I still say the soldier is bad wrong.

To this I stick." More I wouldn't argue. I left the teacher with his eyebrows crawling.

So I'm back to declare there may be hope for you yet. You can plead ignorance. Ignorance pure and simple. The Creator is not stingy with His mercy. Witties are granted compassion, lackers of knowledge given a season to catch up. Is it your fault you missed the wagon? I count it my obligation to set you aright.

Jerb Powell

April Thirteenth

Dear Talt Evarts:

I'm in the worse calamity ever was. The Standing Rock schoolteacher and his bunch are low-rating me amongst the people. They've started a mud ball rolling. They say I vilified you when I pronounced your trip to the Holy Land a snare and a delusion. They howl I'm blaming you for keeping your eyes wide while serving your country. Our transgressor of a postmaster bad-mouthed me with, "All he knows is a chew tobacco."

A sorry come-off for a man to have dirt slung on his name after a life of snatching souls from the Devil's paws. I've strayed seldom from the straight and narrow. I married one woman and clung to her. I never sold my vote. No man has ever been skinned by me, except in a horse trade, and that doesn't count. Aye, the jaspers deserve to swallow their tongues and gag to death.

Pick your ears. Mark me well. I'm not claiming now you didn't go to a country bearing the name "Holy

Land." I'm a fellow with brains enough to turn around when I've learnt I'm heading a wrong direction. What lodges in my craw is the mixing of Up Yonder with a place in this world. I'm willing to allow you visited a town called Jerusalem. I hold it was labeled after the city On High—like Bethlehem, Nebo and Gethsemane here in Kentucky. The Holy Land on earth is the namesake of the Country Above. That you didn't actually go to Glory Land was what I was trying to drive into skulls.

To show I'm of a notion to forgive you, I'll say I hope the cedar lives. Shovel barnyard dirt to it. That will make it walk. It promises to become the hurrah of the mountains, a living sermon, a foretaste of eternal life. I wish I had a sprig of it as a token.

I've been spying into your army record. You were a brave soldier by all my hears. You held your ground square in the whiskers of the foe.

Respectfully,

Jerb Powell

April Seventeenth

Dear Brother Evarts:

The cedar sprig you mailed reached me as green as the olive branch Noah's dove fetched to the ark. I dangled it before the schoolteacher and he threw up his hands and said, "I've hushed." And our postmaster allowed, "If the soldier can overlook your views, I reckon I can." Yes, sir, it takes a while to hammer straight warped minds. I'll hang the sprig over the door where it will feast my eye.

The next occasion I'm over to Wiley Town I'll stop by and shake your hand. I've heard you brought a gill of water from the river called Jordan. Not the really Jordan, of course. A river named after it. I aim to beg a drop or two. And I have a host of questions to ask. A country named for the heavenly one ought to be a pattern for folks living everywhere.

Eternally,

Jerb Powell

BROTHER TO METHUSELUM

HERE on Oak Branch of Ballard Creek we are nearly all kinfolks. We mostly marry amongst ourselves, live and die where we were born, and don't try to run after the rest of the world. Let one of us get twenty or thirty years along, outlast pneumonia fever, typhoid and grippe, we're apt to inhabit this earth a good long spell. Two or three got to be a hundred or so, so agey they looked like dried cushaws. But not another who started living square over again after they had passed the century mark as did Uncle Mize Hardburly. He raised a new set of teeth, grew a full head of hair. Not even John Shell, the oldest man in the world who had his picture in the almanac advertising purgatives, could make this claim. And besides, Uncle Mize's face lost its wrinkles and became as smooth as a June apple.

Uncle Mize was a hundred and three when he began to sprout his hair and teeth. Hair grew back on his noggin as thick as crabgrass in a corn balk. The teeth—they were the really thing. Aye gonnies, it was beyond belief unless you saw them yourself. Gazing into his mouth was akin to peeping into a hollow stump nested with joree eggs. There were the grinders, eyeteeth and incisors. The full set. And was Uncle Mize tickled!

He could stop gumming his tobacco and recommence chewing.

After his rejuvenation, Uncle Mize got to hopping around to beat crickets. He throwed away his spec's. Rarely used them anyhow, except to see how finances stood in his snapping pocketbook. He propped his walkingstick in a corner, for keeps. Aye, I couldn't remember him without that stick which was carved to the appearance of a copperhead snake.

Unnatural it was bound to be, Uncle Mize getting young again and the Hardburly burying ground full of people not nigh so ancient. He had outlived two wives. Nine children awaited final Judgment in the graveyard. His whole family set had gone to Glory, or Torment— who can say?—except two sons, Broadus and Kell. But Uncle Mize took his rebirth like a sheep to green ivy, gammicking over his farm, beating in a crop, cussing and bossing as in younger days. Broadus and Kell hadn't cleared a newground in fifteen seasons. Now, by the hokies! they had to hoist their backsides, whet their shanks, grub and dig. They had to shake hands with a plow handle.

Broadus and Kell were twins, sixty-one years of age, and single. Yet, gosh dog! They couldn't be blamed for not finding doughbeaters when women followed shunning them. They were as alike as churn dashers, homely and tall and stringy, a mite humpbacked, and as common in the face as the Man Above ever shaped and allowed to breathe. As the saying goes, they'd been hit by the ugly stick. How a handsome-looker like Uncle Mize could have sired them beat understanding. Or was there a stranger in the woodpile? O, there were some people sorry enough to think so.

Maw vowed the brothers put her in mind of granny hatchets burrowing in a rotten log, beetle-eyed and nitbrained. Human craney crows, she called them. Why, I don't suppose even a three-time widow would cut eyes at either. Not along Oak Branch, or the whole of Ballard Creek. Not anywhere in the territory. They were willing all right, willing as ferrets in a rabbit hole, but they got nowhere in the marry market. Kell gave up the hunt at around fifty years of age. Broadus never did.

On account of his years, Maw and the other women on Oak were easier on Uncle Mize than on his sons. Nevertheless Uncle Mize had his rakings. They lowrated him partly because he didn't belong to their congregation, didn't pull his chin long as a mule's collar on Sunday. He would go to church—go *at* church, say. He'd loll in the shade of the gilly tree in the yard, and did a preacher step on somebody's toes too hard in the churchhouse, they could steal out and talk with Uncle Mize, swell their chest with the fresh air blowing across Oak from the hickory ridge, and forget about Eternal Damnation. Jawing with Uncle Mize they would presently feel content to wring the pleasures such as they were from this world, and allow the next to rack its own jennies.

I followed hanging after Uncle Mize. You understand how a seventeen-year-old youngster is, big ears and small gumption. Don't know his ankles from a hole in the ground. I relished talk with a speck of seasoning, and Uncle Mize was the fanciest blackguarder in the mountains, slicking the devil's blessings over his tobacco cud, pouring on the vinegar. He could split frog hairs with words. And Uncle Mize was as generous as weather. He'd let me borrow his pocketknife, and most trees on the meeting-ground have my name carved on their trunk. He kept the knife in his snapping pocketbook and sometimes I found money wedged between the blades. Those days I didn't wink at a dime. Even a penny.

So Uncle Mize shunned the rockingchair and got around more. He visited us sometimes despite Maw's disapproval that he was on top of the earth instead of under it. Once she said in his presence, "Hit's unearthly for a body to become young once they've been old. Hit's contrary to prophecy and the plan of creation."

"Cite me," Uncle Mize challenged. "Quote me Scripture on it."

Said Maw, "If it hain't in the Book, it ought to be. O, I've seen plum thickets bloom pretty in a January thaw, and freeze out in February."

"Hazel bushes bust blossoms the first month of the year," Uncle reminded, "and they flourish and endure. It appears the idea of the Almighty for them to flower and beget in winter. And that might sometimes happen in the case of mankind."

Maw had clacked her teeth and hushed. She couldn't outtalk Uncle Mize.

Uncle Mize figured people were jealous. He was reviving, rising again, and they were scared he wasn't mortal. Whether folks will admit to it or not, they want to outlive everybody they know. Especially their enemies. Aye, Uncle Mize didn't account it peculiar, his turning the calendar backwards. "I've aimed to be around a right smart number of years, and I've lived accordingly," he'd say. "I 'stilled my own whiskey, raised my own bread and meat, growed the tobacco I chew, done a mite of everything, and not too much of anything. I split the middle. I've dodged the doctors—the main thing. O, I've had sicknesses, yes sir. But when herbs of my own brewing wouldn't heal, I let the flesh cure itself. And, by the gods, I believe I'm a brother to Methuselum."

Fellows teased Uncle Mize, yet they made small scrimption off of him. He was as foxy as the next'un. They'd inquire was he getting youthful all over, or was it in spots.

"Aye, neighbor," Uncle Mize would cackle. "I'm resurrected from Alpha to Omega, from toe to crown. I'm a match to the apple they call Worldly Wonder. And, hear me, my friends, I'm likely to sire another drove ere there's singing on the point."

"You mean you would wed again?" they would cry.

Uncle Mize would go along with the kidding. "Why, I've married two times in life," he'd banter, "and I might decide to go for twice more—shoe the horse all the way round." But Uncle Mize was talking to hear his head rattle. He didn't have any such business in head.

Uncle Mize kept the buck passing, not allowing it to stick on him, nevertheless, square down, he must of understood he wasn't immortal. Yet he stood in with the best of them, for a while. Now, no, they made nothing off of Uncle Mize. You can't gig a fellow who is laughing harder than you are. It's like spitting into Oak Branch, expecting to hit a fish in the eye. But Bot Shedders, the mail carrier, tried the hardest.

I recollect Uncle Mize got in behind Broadus and Kell and put in a big crop that spring. By hooker-my-crook he planted eleven acres of new-ground corn. Persuading Broadus and Kell to work regular was akin to whooping snakes. Kell was forever hunting a shady spot, Broadus haunting the county seat. Broadus could figure up more reasons for going to town than overalls have pockets. He went to see females riding side-saddle, though his excuses were otherwise. Though he'd never see sixty again, he wouldn't give up pining after the women. I suppose he was hammered together that way. So it took coaxing and begging and cussing on Uncle Mize's part to get the work done. Toward the end of April he had to hire me.

Broadus and Kell set off one morning for the high swag of the ridge to thin and plow corn. I stayed behind to help plant beans in the sass patch. Me and Uncle Mize finished in less than an hour and then lit out for the swag ourselves, hoes across our shoulders. It was a pull, mounting the slope, but Uncle Mize skinned up it as easily as I. We rested on stumps at the top and gazed below at the corn growing black-green and bonny. The blades rustled, the air smelled of tansy. Two crows flopped overhead.

"Be dom," Uncle Mize chuckled, "crows know a master crop when they spot one."

We dropped into the swag through a redbud thicket and made our way to the edge of the field. Broadus and Kell weren't in view. The mule had dragged the plow across the rows and stood biting tops. Uncle Mize flew mad. What he said would rot teeth. Then he hushed and listened. A belch sounded nearby. He grabbed up a sassafras root and tickle-toed toward the noise.

Broadus and Kell were stretched behind a dead chestnut, a fruit jar between them, drunk as hooty-owls. Kell slept peacefully while his brother dropped anty mars down his collar. Beading an eye on Uncle Mize, Broadus lifted the jar and said, "Come take you a sup, Pap, and loosen up your whistle."

Uncle Mize swung the sassafras. It zizzed, breaking the jar to smithereens. Broadus sprang to his feet, aiming to high-tail it, but Uncle Mize brought the root against his skull full force, and it wasn't a pulled lick either. Broadus laid over, cold as clabber. Kell must of dreamt there was a war broke out, for he staggered up, threshed his arms, and when he saw who was there, grumbled,

"What you acting so brigetty about, Pap?" Uncle Mize answered with a blow of the root, and Kell could only crouch and fend off the whacks.

On untwisting the mule's harness, Uncle Mize started plowing himself, busting middles, geeing and hawing, and I tried to keep ahead in the row, thinning stalks, but I couldn't. He worked like a twenty-year-old, like a whiteback. And he had the field cultivated by dinner time. He finished it snorting worse than the mule. I saw Uncle Mize was trembly. I saw the wings of his nose and the tags of his ears were pale. The plowing had hurt him, had set him back considerable. He had overdone.

Uncle Mize took the punies. He moped about the house, satisfied to reclaim his walkingstick and rocking-chair. He wasn't so branfired fiesty thereafter. He would holler to folks going Oak Branch road and invite them to come in and gab with him. He didn't have to beckon Bot Shedders. Bot regularly stopped his mail hack and retailed gossip an hour or so.

Bot was company for Uncle Mize, with me in the fields trying to conquer weeds, and Broadus and Kell piddling. Broadus and Kell! Be there a shady row, it would take them half a day to hoe it. They made friends with the crabgrass, it appeared. They left standing more than they slew.

Well, we'd go in for dinner and find Bot telling some winding yarn that would redden the face of a Frankfort lawyer. I wouldn't believe Bot Shedders on his deathbed.

Bot would stay for dinner usually, and I'll be dad-burned if he wasn't a bigger eater than liar. I've seen him down a half-gallon of buttermilk, a bowl of shucky beans, two potato onions, and four breakings of corn-bread at a sitting.

One day I heard Bot tell Uncle Mize something off-handedly. He glanced at the old witch of a cousin who did the cooking and said, "Uncle Mizey, you ought to get you a woman to pretty up the house. Be it I was single, and turning back the calendar, it's plime-blank what I'd do."

"Talk sense, old son," Uncle Mize threw back, without smiling. And that was the first I knew he wasn't for joshing any more. It figured. The plowing had undone him.

Bot pulled a dry face. "A man needs a woman to snip the hair out of his ears and keep his toenails trimmed."

"Ruther to own a redbone hound," Uncle Mize said. "When I get easement, I'm apt to take up fox hunting again, the sport that used to pleasure me. I'll spend nights in the hills, listening to the music."

Bot grunted. "It's to be expected a man would lose his courage after he passed the hundred mark. Hit must make a parcel of difference. Even seventy-five might be the cut-off for some, and at eighty the fire is out shorely."

To this Uncle Mize said grumpily, "You have no fashion of knowing until you're there yourself."

"I was a-guessing," Bot said. "Speculating. But I've

sort of a notion you've crossed the river. That rocker has captured you for good."

"I have as much man-courage left as airy a person on Oak," Uncle Mize declared. "The fact is, women don't trip themselves up running to marry the oldest feller this side of the Book of Genesis."

"Any day you want to," Bot said, "you can order a woman. If you own property, have a few dollars in pocket, it'll draw'em like yellow jackets to a stir-off."

"I've never heard tell of such," said Uncle Mize. Bot was such a fibber, who could believe him?

"Upon my honor, you can order a woman through a newspaper."

Bot's stomach got to shaking, but he managed to hold his face in check.

"I've no mind to order a woman for myself," Uncle Mize answered, thinking this was another of Bot's big ones, "but, by the hokies, I'd do anything to locate wives for Broadus and Kell."

Following that, Bot Shedders handled affairs to suit his own notion, without even saying 'chicken butter' to anybody. He stopped by daily, and when I'd come in he'd be jabbering. And it got to where he would laugh at nothing at all. You might say, "Git," to a dog, or, "The moon'll be full tonight," and he'd double up. He might bust out with nobody saying anything. Yet a month passed before I caught on. One noon when I walked in from the fields there sat Bot with a mess of letters. I'd never beheld so many to one person—sixteen by count. He reported they were for Uncle Mize, and Uncle Mize was staring at them and hadn't cracked an envelope.

"Who do you figure wrote them?" Uncle Mize inquired.

"Why, Uncle," Bot explained, "these are from women craving a husband. Craving a man the worst way."

Uncle Mize glared at Bot. For once Bot had told the truth. "Where did they get the idee I wanted a wife?"

"I put your name in the papers. Just you looky here." Bot drew a newspaper clipping from his billfold and read aloud: "Oldest Man in Kentucky Seeks Wife."

"Well, well, well," Uncle Mize breathed, and then he said, "Open and read some of their scratching."

Bot ripped the lid off a letter, reading it to himself first. He got to laughing, gagging like a calf with a cob in its throat. He forgot to spit, and ambeer dribbled his chin.

"Reading must be a slow and tickling business," Uncle Mize gibed. "What's the hold up?"

"This one's from Georgia," Bot cackled. "Says she's seventy-two, been a widow forty years, doesn't paint her lips or dye her hair, and keeps a clean house. Says she wants to spend her remaining days of grace with a mate."

"She sounds decent," Uncle Mize allowed, "but she's along in age. Too old for me. A woman ripens quicker'n a man."

"Ah," Bot chuckled, "if it's a pullet you want, maybe

she's here somewheres." He ripped more envelopes, glimpsing at the pages, saying at last, "Here's a girl from Oklahoma who is sixteen. Says her step-paw spanks her for wearing high heels and twigging her hair, and she intends to run away from home. Says she has eternally dreamed of marrying a mountain man, age no hinder. And she signs, Gobs of kisses, Suzie."

"Well, coon my dogs!" Uncle Mize blurted. "I hain't going to rob a cradle. No, sir."

Bot wanted to rip more, but Uncle Mize claimed he'd heard all the reading he could abide for one day. Since the plowing he tired easily. "That Suzie," said he, "ought to have the spankings poured on the harder. Was I her pappy, I'd draw blisters with one hand, bust'em with the other." Then he said, "I don't believe I'll marry, and none of them to now seem fit for Broadus and Kell either. Too elderly, too young, none in betwixt."

"My opinion, Broadus wouldn't be choosy," Bot said. "Anyhow, the letters have barely started coming. You'll have a square pick of the world."

The puny spell hung on. Uncle Mize stayed several days in bed. He was up and down all June and July, drinking cherrybark tea to strengthen his blood, a rag on his chest smeared with groundhog grease for his wind. He wasn't in pain, just weak, sluggish, no account. Bot Shedders stopped by every mail day, keeping peg on Uncle Mize's health, delivering more letters. For Uncle Mize he was a right smart company.

O, I reckon it was dull for Uncle Mize the days the mail didn't run, and with me and Broadus and Kell in the fields. Or me in the fields working by my lone, Kell asleep under a bush, and Broadus at the county seat. Time can hang heavy as a steelyard pea. Flat on his back, I expect a man will do a lot of cogitation. It might have caused Uncle Mize to take a fancy to one of the letters. For days handrunning Uncle Mize would say to Bot, "Bohannon"—that was Bot's really name—"read that there letter again," and Bot would know which one.

"Says her name is Olander Spence," Bot would say. "Says she lives in Perry County, not more'n twenty miles from Oak Branch. Says she's fifty-five November coming, and tuck loving care of her pappy till he died, the reason she never married. Says she can cook to suit any stomach, says she washes clothes so white you'd swear dogwoods bloomed around the house on Mondays. And listen! Says she can trash any man hoeing a row of corn."

The letter pleased Uncle Mize. It livened him more than the cherrybark tea, or the greasy rag. A day arrived when he said, "I've settled on the idea I do need a woman fiddling around the house, waiting on me, and hewing out the garden. The hours get teejous counting cracks in the ceiling and listening to the roosters crow. The Perry County woman sounds smart and clever, not afraid to bend her elbows. I've decided to have her fetched."

When Uncle Mize took a notion to do a thing, he

was all grit and go. As with the plowing, he got into a fidgit, and if he hadn't been plagued by weakness he would have mounted a horse and traveled to Perry County himself. Or if the corn hadn't been overtaken by crabgrass and foxtail, he might have sent me. Broadus and Kell swore and be-damned if they would go. Kell put his number twelve shoe down flat. "I'm here," he made oath, "and I'm not moving." Kell was too lazy to kill a snake anyhow. Broadus said, "Hain't my wedding nor funeral. I might bring a woman for myself, but I'll do no wife-hauling for another."

Either Broadus or Kell plime-blank had to make tracks. Uncle Mize swore their breeches wouldn't hold shucks if they didn't make up their minds which. When they held out against all argument, he touched on their weakness. They wouldn't shun money. He drew a taw line in the yard and set them playing crack-o-loo. He fished two silver dollars out of his snapping pocketbook for bait. "Farthest from the line goes to Perry County," he decreed, "and both can keep the dollar."

Broadus pitched, coming close to the mark. Kell took a hair sighting, aiming like measuring death, and beat him; he straddled the line with the U.S. eagle. Broadus let in cussing, but he started getting his readies on. Uncle Mize jumped lively for a change, fixing the saddle-bags, bridling two horses. Broadus set off, giving the animals their heads, letting them take their sweet time. Being poky was his revenge.

It was a Tuesday that Broadus started for Perry

County, and had he returned the following day there would have been a wedding in the middle of the week. Forty miles should have worked out to a day-and-a-half trip. Kell saw to the marriage license. Those years you didn't need your blood 'tasted,' and you could send for the knot-tieing document. El Caney Rowan, the preacher, came to do the hitching, and along trotted Elihu DeHart. Where you see Elihu you see his fiddle, and him itching to play. Folks within walking distance came. Most everybody on Oak Branch except Maw. Some rode over from Ballard, Snaggy, and Lairds Creek.

But Broadus didn't show up. I hadn't supposed he would make a bee-line, being he had gone against his will and want. Broadus's head was as hard as a hicker nut. People waited, the day stretched, and no Broadus. I kept thinking of the crabgrass crowding the corn, the knee high foxtail, and me wasting time. Late afternoon arrived, the cows lowed at the milk gap, the calves bawled. The sun dropped, and folks had to go home frustrated.

I didn't get my natural sleep that night. Uncle Mize sprung a pain in his chest, and I had to sit up with him. I heated a rock to lay to his heart; I boiled coffee strong enough to float wedges; I drew bucket after bucket of fresh well water to cool his brow. He eased about daylight and before I could sneak a nap for myself, aye gonnies, if folks didn't start coming back, only more of them. Overnight the word had spread further still.

People turned up from Burnt Ridge and Flat Gap,

from Cain Creek, and from as far away as Smacky and Sporty Creek. Oak Branch emptied out totally—even Maw. Maw's curiosity got stronger than her religion. People waded the yard and weeds led a hard life. A pity they couldn't have tramped the balks of Uncle Mize's corn.

Uncle Mize ate common at breakfast: two hoe cakes, butter and molasses, a slice of cob-smoked ham. Then he went onto the porch and people crowded to pump his hand, the men sniggering fit to choke, the women giggling behind handkerchers. Elihu struck up "Old Joe Clark" on his fiddle, and Uncle Mize cut three steps rusty to prove his limberness. I knew Uncle Mize wasn't up to it though. His cheeks were ashen, his ears tallow. After he'd wrung every hand within reach he told me he aimed to go inside and rest a bit, and for me to rouse him the first knowledge I had of Broadus.

In the neighborhood of eleven o'clock I heard a yelp and glanced toward the bend of the road, and there did come Broadus. You couldn't hear the *clop* of hoofs for the rattle of voices. Folks hung over the fence; they stood tiptoe; they stretched their necks. There came Broadus astride the first horse, leading the second. And nobody rode the second animal. On shading my eyes I discovered the woman sitting behind him, riding sidesaddle.

Bot Shedders cracked, "That other nag must of gone lame, or throwed a shoe. No female ever sot that close to Broadus Hardburly."

I hustled to Uncle Mize's room. The door was shut. I poked a finger through the hole and lifted the latch, calling as I entered. There was no reply. The shade was pulled and the room dusty dark. I waited until my eyes adjusted and then I saw Uncle Mize flat on the bed, his breeches and socks on. I started to shake him, but I didn't. I couldn't. Not a sound came from him. He wasn't breathing. I stood frozen a moment, then I skittered off to bring Kell. Kell reacted as I did, scared and shaky. We took a long solid look at Uncle Mize, and it was the truth. He wasn't with us any more.

"Let's tell Broadus," Kell said. We closed the door, not speaking a word to anybody. Broadus had ridden in at the wagon gate and was helping Olander Spence to the ground. I saw right then Uncle Mize had made a good choice. Olander Spence seemed not too bad a looker, and her hands were big and thick and used to work. Her buck teeth were as white as hens' eggs.

Broadus unbuckled the saddles and flung them onto the woodpile. He said to the Spence woman, "You sit here on the chopblock while I stable and feed the horses."

We walked into the barn, Broadus, Kell and me. They opened the stall doors while I climbed up into the loft for hay, and when I came down Kell had told his brother.

"He blowed out like a candle," Kell explained.

Broadus leaned against the wall, his mouth open.

Kell grumbled, "That brought-on woman has got us

into a mess of trouble. A pure picklement. You fetched her here, and you're the one to take her back home."

Broadus shook his bur of a head. He wasn't much for telling his business, but now he had to. "She hain't going nowheres," he said. "Me and her done some marrying yesterday."

Broadus and Kell latched the stall doors and hung up the bridles. They went toward the house, and I just stood there. I didn't want to go back into the room where Uncle Mize was. I felt like cutting down a tree, or splitting a cord of wood—anything to brush my mind off of Uncle Mize. I got me a hoe, slipped behind the barn, and on to the farthest field. I slew an acre of crabgrass before sundown.

THE SCRAPE

I was walking up Ballard Creek and reckoning to myself that foxes were abroad and sparking on such a night when I happened upon Jiddy Thornwell sprawled in the road at the mouth of Sporty Hollow. Though the moon was low and the ridges in shadow, there was enough light to yellow the ground along the creek.

On seeing Jiddy I expected to tickle-toe past and go on to the square dance at Enoch Lovern's where I'd headed. I was traveling late on purpose to dodge rowdies of his ilk. A body with the gumption of a gnat wouldn't fool time in his company, for if ever one was routed to burning Torment, he was the jasper. Fractious and easily riled, and as folks say, too mean to live. Then I bethought myself. I couldn't allow any man to get his neck broken by a wheel or brains stepped in by a nag. An unworthy way to perish. Anyhow, being drunk, he'd have a bottle on him, and after borrowing a gill I'd skeedaddle.

I gave Jiddy a poke with my shoe. He moved a speck and cracked his eyelids. He sat up and made to yawn. And I saw there wasn't much if any whiskey in him, and I knew something was afoot, something to nobody's good.

"Jiddy," I chided, "what the hoot are you doing sleeping in the road?"

He laughed, and jumped up. He had been shamming. Without a doubt he had spotted me before I did him. He aimed to test what I'd do.

"You were laying pretty to have your skull cracked," I jabbered, slapping his pockets. I felt no bottle, just a knife and the 32-squeeze-trigger he regularly packed. When sober, Jiddy wasn't too prickly and overbearing. You could horse around with him. "I've seen cha-racters blind drunk acting with more sanity," said I.

Jiddy inquired where I was headed, and I answered, "Where do you reckon?" Except to attend the square dance at Enoch Lovern's what other reason would either of us have to be on the Ballard road of a Saturday night? He was talking to hear his head rattle. I cautioned, "If you're wanting more than a couple of sashays with Posey, you'd better get a hump on. You're already late."

Jiddy had been sparking Woots Houndshell's daughter for near on to a year but lately Cletis Wilhoyt had been cutting in on him. In headstrongness and pride, Cletis and Jiddy were fair matches. Put them both in a poke and shake it, and it would be a question which would pop out first. Well, I'll confess to it. I was soft on Posey Houndshell myself. Yet I'm no witty, no dumb-head. I believed three's a crowd, and especially when it included these two gents.

"I'm waiting on Cletis Wilhoyt," Jiddy said. "We aim

to settle some business tonight. Settle it for all time coming, hereinafter and forever. The winner might travel to Houndshell's, be he in shape to. You're our eyewitness, the prover neither of us bushwhacked the other."

"Gosh dog!" I blustered, and then, "Uh-uh. You're not talking to me. I'm a short spell here." The boilers of hell would explode did this pair lock horns. Hard numbers, the both. Stubborn as peavies. Fellows who don't care whether it snows oats or rains tomcats, they're dangerous to be around. The preachers say what's written to happen will come to pass, whether or no. But I didn't count it my duty to stand by and eyeball this showdown. Hell-o, no!

"Everything is fixed," Jiddy said, not listening. "Cletis swore he'd meet me when the moon is up plumb." He cocked his chin and sighted the moon-ball. "She's low, the old sister, but she's climbing." He grinned. "We'll have what the almanac calls 'useful moonlight.'" And he said, "You'll view a fight that will make the records."

"Yeah," chuffed I, "the courthouse records," and I complained, "Are you figuring I'm going to referee a shooting match? I wasn't born on Crazy Creek, recollect. Bullets are like horses' hooves, they don't have eyes."

Jiddy said, "Pistols are for the chickenhearted, and that's not our case. Not mine or Cletis's. We'll manage otherwise."

"Dadburn it, Jid," I ranted, "you're an idjit if you think I'm mixing in your and Cletis' scrapes. Where do I profit? Sheriffs, summonses, roosting in the witness chair, a big rigmaroar. Aye, no. I've been here, and I'm done gone." Yet you didn't leave Jiddy until it suited his notion. Not unless you wanted your hair parted with his 32-squeeze-trigger.

"Let's round us up a drink," smoothed Jiddy. "Shade Muldraugh has an operation on Rope Works, yon side of the ridge. What say we make a raid on him?"

"Shade's likker is the worst in Baldridge County," I faulted. "The sorriest since Adam made apple-jack. Why, he can't even boil water without scorching it." But I might as well have been talking to a mule.

Jiddy declared, "Whatever Shade is distilling, we'll down. Tonight we'll cull nothing. Pass nothing by."

We set off. Legging it up the ridge I juggled plans in my head to shake off Jiddy, and in a fashion which would leave me blameless. We mounted by knee and main strength, climbing ground so steep you'd nearly skin your nose, and emerged in a clearing where moonlight made blossom the hazel bushes. Jiddy told me to stay there, he'd prospect a bit. I heard twigs snapping for a while, then the heavy breathing of the Muldraugh bull in the valley. A fox barked, an answering yap followed. It was a lonesomey place and I longed to hightail it. But I bethought myself: who at the dance would bother to cut eyes at me? All the girls I fancied were spoken for, Posey Houndshell included. Well, I'd get away from Jiddy in due course. Not just yet. It wasn't good sense to.

Presently I heard Jiddy's squeeze-trigger pop and I dropped flat on the ground, and I stayed flat until I heard leaves rattling and Jiddy walked out of the woods.

"What happened?" I choked, picturing Shade Muldraugh with a bullet in his gizzard, his toes curled.

"Ah, I let off my gun to scare him," said Jiddy. "And did he skeedaddle! Aye gonnies, you could of shot dice on his shirttail." And Jiddy said, "Come on. We'll take our pleasure."

We footed along a bench of land some three hundred yards, and of a sudden there it was in a pocket of a cliff. Muldraugh's works were hid as clever as a guinea's nest, and I doubt I could have spotted it at twenty feet even in broad daylight. Although a fire burned under the pot, the steam wasn't yet up. The worm hadn't begun to driddle.

The lack of the finished product didn't faze Jiddy. He leaned over the tub of still-beer and scooped a gourd dipper full. He drained it, my belly retching at the sight. Then he dipped up a second. I never could swallow such stuff myself. It's sour as whigs. Causes a wild head and too many trips to the White House. "Quit guzzling that slop," I grumbled. "Hit would stop a goat."

Unless you 'funnel it,' the beer hasn't much power, and Jiddy funneled. He took loose the wire the dipper hung by and thrashed his leg with it as if forcing himself.

Finally I said, "Hell's bangers, Jid! Lay off and I'll locate some really stuff, pure corn, the old yellow kind." A big-eyed lie on my part. Nobody made such spirits any more. All you could find was who-shot. But it wasn't merely the beer, or my wanting to vomit watching him that made me promise it. I had finally hatched a scheme.

After a sighting of the moon, Jiddy agreed. She was fully an hour from high. First, he peed into the beer, not that you could nasty it worse than it was. We dropped down the ridge to the Ballard road and back-tracked a piece to Pawpaw Branch, Jiddy thrashing his leg with the wire, spurring himself it seemed. "Now," says I, "you do the waiting." Epp Clevenger wouldn't have pardoned me for bringing such a character along. What I'd decided to do was to get Jiddy hoot-owl drunk. With the beer already in him, an easy matter according to my calculations. A few gills of really likker would serve. He'd pass out, and I would scoot.

Epp had a run on and when I came up he was acting mighty uncomfortable. My rattling rocks approaching his furnace had near panicked him. After recognizing me he cried, "Son of a dog! Why didn't you holler, say who you was?" He had to sit five minutes to let his heart stop knocking. He sold me a short-quart on credit, fresh-run, hot from the worm. Bad stuff, he would of admitted. Epp wasn't guaranteeing nothing. Though winded by the climb, I started back directly. The moon wasn't slowing, so I couldn't either. I raced her, you might say.

Well, s'r, when I reached Jiddy the beer hadn't touched him. And he had imbibed nigh on to a half-gallon, the least. A few slugs would of put me under for a day, provided it stayed down. But I've heard it claimed, no matter how much you drink, if you don't want to get drunk, you won't. Beginning to get nervous, I handed Jiddy the bottle, and though it wasn't agey or yellow or pure corn as I'd promised, he upped it and didn't grumble. I skipped it myself, for it had a whang of coal oil and lye, and the pig shorts in the mash didn't recommend it. I eyed Jiddy pulling at the bottle. I watched the moon-ball soar.

The moon took off like Lindbergh. The old sister was flying, and if anything, the more Jiddy drank the soberer he became. Never saw the beat. If Epp Clevenger was fidgity, you ought to of seen me. Hardly a fourth of the whiskey was gone when the moon peaked. The valley lit up wholly, the waters of Ballard shimmered. The ridges were lumpy with trees. And there came Cletis Wilhoyt walking.

I trotted to meet Cletis, vowing to him none would gain in a ruckus between him and Jiddy. Woots Houndshell's Posey would slam the door on the both of them when she heard. I even made up a rumor she had already dropped Jiddy like a hot nail, and he didn't need to bother. For my trouble I got called a bad name, and told to go drown myself. That was Cletis. Mean as a horsefly.

There I was between hell and a flint stone. Come a

thousand years I couldn't have changed their minds. Their heads were as hard as ball-peen hammers. And this was to be no fair fist scrap either, no mere knockdown combat, with the one who hollered 'gate post' first the loser. There would be no pausing, no blow counted foul. Win or perish, endure or die. And gosh dog! They weren't even mad. They talked chin to chin, plotting the battle, cool as moss. By now I was in possession of the bottle and I made up for time lost. Coal oil, lye and pig shorts didn't stop me.

Jiddy called me over to them and gave me his 32-squeeze-trigger. Cletis surrendered an old German luger. The luger was as neat a handgun as ever I fingered. I laid the weapons on a rock. Jiddy produced a wire— the wire he'd packed from Muldraugh's works. He had it doubled in his hippocket. He ordered me to tie an end around his left wrist, and the other about Cletis'. A thing they had agreed on. I did what I was bid do. I bound them to their satisfaction, skin-tight. Next I was asked to treat them to a drink. As Cletis tipped the bottle I noted his face was the color of the air. Following him, Jiddy took a long pull. His countenance—aye, I can't describe it. I recollect his eyes flicked like a wren's tail.

Then Jiddy told me to stand clear. I retreated a couple or three yards. "Farther, farther," ordered Jiddy, and I was stumbling backwards crawdabber fashion when I saw them clasp left hands, and fish in pockets for knives with their right. They opened the knives with their teeth. I saw arms raise and metal glint. It was that moony. My heart didn't knock. It plain quit.

Cletis struck first, as I recall, swinging outward, elbow angling, and had there been a wind the blade would have whistled. I heard a rip like an ax cleaving the limb of a tree. I froze, and I couldn't have moved had the hills come toppling. The span of Jiddy's back hindered my view, and I couldn't swear for certain, but I figured Cletis' knife had split him wide. Yet Jiddy only grunted and plunged his blade as if to sever the key-notch of an oak. Cletis rocked and gurgled. Cletis gurgled like water squiggling in the ground during rainy weather. They kept to their feet, backing and filling, breathing as heavily as Muldraugh's bull had, arms rising and striking. And they kept on striking.

I've seen rams butt skulls till it thundered. I've witnessed caged wildcats tear hide. Neither was a scrimption to this. My body grew roots. My legs were posts without joints. I went off the hinges, I reckon. I begged Jiddy and Cletis to quit. I pled, I bellowed. I shouted till I couldn't utter a croak, and then I covered my eyes and fell down bawling. Since my child days I'd shed few tears, and these came rough. They set my eyeballs afire.

After a spell I quieted. I cracked my lids and peeped out. Jiddy and Cletis were laying alongside each other in the road, laying as stiff as logs. At night red is black, and there was black over and around them. They lay in a gore of black. And the next thing I knew I was running up Ballard Creek. I might have run all the way to Enoch Lovern's if the short-quart hadn't slipped from under my belt. I grabbed it up and threw it winding. It bounced along the ruts ahead and never busted. When I got up to the bottle I hoisted **it** and drained it to the bottom.

I didn't run any more. I walked, and as I walked I calmed. What was done was done. Predestination, church folks call it. I footed along peart, thinking of what Jiddy had said once about wanting to be buried in a chestnut coffin so he would go through hell a-popping, and I thought about something else. I thought about Posey Houndshell. Nobody stood between me and her.

ENCOUNTER ON KEG BRANCH

"You know Adam Claiborne over to Thacker? I mean the welfare Adam who works for the government. Well, sir, I'm wanting to send him some word by you. And I want you to write it down as I say it so you'll get it straight. Tell him that me and that woman has done quit each other and living apart and I want him to see her and learn what she's got to talk about. Tell him not to specify anything. And tell Adam I want to see him on particular business before the next court sets. Tell him to be slick, be slick in his business.

"They swore out a crazy warrant for me, her and her sister. They had me put in jail a spell. Her and her sister, biggest fools of women ever I seed. I aim to damn'em every chance I get. She's living with another man, been living with him three months. He's got her bigged. Tell Adam to not let nothing out. Tell Adam to specify we hain't married, by God. I aim to down that woman. Aim to have her sent to the asylum. Aye, she's been there before. The man she's living with, he's been there too. I aim to shock him next. A shame-scandal! Her sister tore her dress and swore rape on me—me at my age, seventy-one, and on the old-age draw. Had me put in jail. She told enough lies on me to send her to hell.

"I lived with that woman seven years and she thinks we're married. Why, we drawed up a little old paper and she didn't know any differ. That's how much a dumb-head she is. People like her ought to have their heads pinched off when they're born.

"I tell you, they don't know nothing, her and her sister. Nary a one can tell their age. Upon my honor, they don't know what day it is until the school bus runs. Her mother before her couldn't of told how old she was either. The whole drove, they don't know dirt from goose manure. Yet lie! They can lie like a dog a-trotting. They'll get before the county judge over to Thacker and they'll pop their hands and tell the biggest ones ever was.

"I'm building me a house on Short Fork. Tell Adam Claiborne that. The reason I've just come from Bee Tree. Bee Tree is the next hollow to Short Fork, and Short Fork is over yonder ridge. Well, s'r, I was over on Bee Tree and I saw another woman. A widow-woman. She's older'n me, five to seven years. She didn't tell me but she has the looks of it. She says, 'I want to get married,' and I says, 'I do too.' So I'm building me a house and I'm going to put her in it."

GLOSSARY

a-b-abs, alphabet
airy, any
allus, always
anty mar, ant
aye gonnies, I'll bet guineas
   (gold)

backing and filling, back and
   forth
Bad Man, Devil
bait, enough
ball-peen hammer, round-head
   hammer for beating metal
Big Thick, unabridged dictionary
blow-George, liar, compulsive
   talker, also metal cover for
   encouraging a draft in the
   fireplace
Book, Holy Bible
brigetty, ill-humored
bull hole, bottomless hole into
   which defeated candidates are
   reputed to jump

cap corn, heat corn until it bursts
chinch bug, bedbug
chinebone, backbone
chub (cherub), baby
crab, grumble
crack-o-loo, pitch-penny game
crawdabber, crayfish
crazy warrant, affidavit of
   insanity
Crossbar Hotel, jail

devil's snuff box, puffball mush-
   room
diddles, baby chickens
doughbeater, wife
dram, drink
draw skims, make misty
driddle, dribble
drummer, traveling salesman

fit, fight
flats, bedbugs
follow, to make a habit of
force put, a necessity
frog skin, dollar bill

gammicking, frolicking
gate post, surrender
gig, josh
gilly tree, Balm of Gilead
gob smoke, smoke from burning
   mine refuse
gom, mess
granny-doctor, midwife
granny hatchet, lizard
gum of bees, beehive

hand-pie, fruit-filled puff
haw, hawthorn
hay doodle, hay stack
hit, it
hook, steal
horse apple, variety of apple,
   also horse dung
hump, hurry

imp, imitate

jake-walking, partial paralysis caused by imbibing ginger-flavored spirits
Jape, Japanese
jasper, unworthy person, also wasper (wasp)
jillion, a countless number
johnny-walkers, stilts
joree, towhee
jowl, jaw

Law, officer of the Law
limber-jim, hickory switch

master time, great occasion

old age draw, old age pension
Old Christmas, Epiphany, January 6
Old Horny, Devil
Old Nine, brand name for twist tobacco
ontelling, unknown

particulars, sex organs
peavey, lever used in handling logs
pen-hooker, cattle trader
piddling, dawdling
pieded (pied), spotted
pig shorts, by-product in milling grain
plime-blank, exactly
poke, bag
poll, head
potty, belly
puck (pucker), contract into folds

quiet-Bob, silent

rabbit lick, blow with the side of the hand to the base of the neck
rag off the bush, fly into a rage
reading hands, fortune telling
rigamaroar, uproar

saddle of the gap, middle
sashay, strut
sass, vegetables
scrimption, the smallest bit
Serpent, Devil
shakes, shingles
sharp tack, wiseacre
shorts, bran, husks of grain
si-goggling, tilted, off-balance
Silver War, American Civil War
singing on the point, funeral
spark, to court
stalking horse, candidate put forward to divide the opposition
stir-off, molasses making
sugartop, inferior whiskey
sweetbreads, spleen

'tater-hole, hide
teejous, tedious
tip, touch, handle
Torment, hell
turnkey, person in charge of prison's keys, jailor

wasper (wasp), unworthy person
whanker, in line
whet, small amount
whiteback, downy woodpecker
white-eye, avoid work
White House, privy
who-shot, low grade whiskey
witty, fool

This book has been set
& printed in Janson with Centaur
used for display by Heritage Printers, Inc.
for Gnomon Press
P.O. Box 106
Frankfort
Kentucky
40602